T0287082

PRAISE FOR *DEAD SWEET*

WINNER of the Blackbird Award for Best Icelandic Crime Debut

'Within the slick storyline, the author manages to draw exceptional and realistic characters who are faced with terrible crimes ... The book hooks you in from the very first page and keeps you there right until the unexpected ending, which puts the whole story in a new light' Blackbird Award judges: Yrsa Sigurðardóttir, Ragnar Jónasson, Bjarni Þorsteinsson

'A breathtaking political thriller from one of Iceland's most exciting new voices' Eva Björg Ægisdóttir

'Katrín Júlíusdóttir skilfully weaves together family dynamics, dark pasts and criminal endeavours in this masterful narrative' Lilja Sigurðardóttir

'*Dead Sweet* is a book that is hard to put down once you start reading it ... An excellent debut thriller with a highly original storyline' Sæunn Gísladóttir, The Reading Room

'It's no surprise that Katrin received the Blackbird Award this year ... a well-written thriller' *Morgunblaðið*

'Keeps you intrigued and maintains a high tempo until the last page' Már Másson Maack, City of Literature / Literature Web

ABOUT THE AUTHOR

Katrín Júlíusdóttir is a former Icelandic politician, elected in 2003 and serving as Minister of Industry, Energy and Tourism, Minister of Finance and Economy and Social Democratic Alliance's vice-chair until she retired from politics in 2016. Before she was elected to parliament, Katrín was an advisor and project manager at a tech company and a senior buyer and CEO in the retail sector, as well as the managing director of a student union. She studied anthropology and has also received an MBA. She was managing director of Finance Iceland from 2016-2022.

Katrín won the Blackbird Award for best Icelandic crime debut for her first novel, *Dead Sweet*, in 2020, and it received immense critical acclaim, hitting the bestseller lists shortly after publication. Katrín was raised in Kópavogur, about fifteen minutes' drive from downtown Reykjavík, and she now lives in the neighbouring town of Garðabær with her family. She is married to author Bjarni M. Bjarnason, who encouraged her to start writing, and they have four sons.

Follow Katrín on X @katrinjul, facebook.com/katrin.julius dottir and Instagram @katrinjuliusdottir.

ABOUT THE TRANSLATOR

A series of unlikely coincidences allowed Quentin Bates to escape English suburbia as a teenager with the chance of a gap year working in Iceland. For a variety of reasons, the year stretched to become a gap decade, during which time he went native in the north of Iceland, acquiring a new language, a new profession and a family.

He is the author of a series of crime novels set in present-day Iceland. His translations include works by Guðlaugur Arason, Ragnar Jónasson, Einar Kárason and Sólveig Pálsdóttir, as well as Lilja Sigurðardóttir's Reykjavík Noir trilogy, standalone novel *Betrayal* and the Áróra series. Follow Quentin on Twitter @graskeggur.

DEAD SWEET

Katrín Júlíusdóttir
Translated by Quentin Bates

ORENDA
BOOKS

Orenda Books
16 Carson Road
West Dulwich
London SE21 8HU
www.orendabooks.co.uk

First published in the United Kingdom by Orenda Books 2023
Originally published in Icelandic as *Sykur* by Veröld, 2020
Copyright © Katrín Júlíusdóttir 2020
English translation © Quentin Bates 2023

A catalogue record for this book is available from the British Library.

Hardback ISBN 978-1-914585-99-9
Paperback ISBN 978-1-916788-17-6
eISBN 978-1-914585-31-9

The publication of this translation has been made possible
through the financial support of

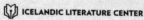 ICELANDIC LITERATURE CENTER

Typeset in Garamond by typesetter.org.uk

Printed and bound by CPI Group (UK) Ltd, Croydon CR0 4YY

For sales and distribution, please contact info@orendabooks.co.uk

PRONUNCIATION GUIDE

Icelandic has a couple of letters that don't exist in other European languages and which are not always easy to replicate. The letter ð is generally replaced with a d in English, but we have decided to use the Icelandic letter to remain closer to the original names. Its sound is closest to the hard th in English, as found in *thus* and *bathe*.

The letter r is generally rolled hard with the tongue against the roof of the mouth. In pronouncing Icelandic personal and place names, the emphasis is placed on the first syllable.

Agnar – Ak-narr
Akranes – Aa-kra-ness
Arnar – Ard-naar
Daði – Dah-thee
Dóra – Doe-ra
Einar – Ay-nar
Elín – El-yn
Erla – Aird-la
Eyjafjallajökull – Ey-ya-fyat-la-jeok-utl
Garðar – Gahr-thar
Guðrún – Guth-ruen
Guðmundur – Guth-mund-uur
Gunnar – Gunn-nar
Halla – Hat-la
Helgi – Hel-kee

Ingólfur – Ink-ohl-voor
Kópavogur – Koe-pa-voe-goor
Ómar – Oh-mar
Óttar – Oht-tar
Sigurdís – Sig-oor-dees
Stefanía – Steh-fan-ee-a
Thorgeir – Thor-gayr
Thrúður – Throo-thur
Unnar – Oon-nar
Viktor – Vikh-tor

DEAD SWEET

PROLOGUE

My head's bursting and my body feels so heavy that I can't lift a finger. Is it because I'm soaked? Waves break over me. The salt stings. My head rests against smooth, cold rock. Everything is going numb, and I can barely feel my body now. It doesn't look like I'll be able to find my way out of here by myself. If I'm lucky, someone will turn up.

Can't stand up. No idea how long I've been here. It feels like a lifetime, but might be no more than a quarter of an hour. Have I been awake the whole time? I suppose I deserve this. I've done pretty well for myself, but I've not treated the people around me particularly kindly ... Mum! She'll call soon, surely? She normally checks up on me before bedtime. She never stops worrying about me. Old habits die hard, I guess. Sometimes I can't tell if she's shielding me from the world, or protecting the world from me. I hope someone sees me here.

I can hear flies, like fighter jets in the distance. Waves break over me, but I still can't move. So this is what it's like, having no control; being between life and death. It's sensing that something is going very wrong with your body, but not knowing what, and not being able to do a single thing about it. That heat at the back of my head must be a swelling. Unless it's blood. The blow was so heavy, crushing. Then there was the kicking. How many kicks did I get? I need to get away from this place, get myself fixed up. I've often made people angry. But never like that. The fury was colossal, overflowing with hatred.

The sky seems to be getting darker. The gloom deepening. But it isn't because of the dimming of the sun. It's because life is fading away.

My life.

Erla was up early on the day of the party. She'd had a sleepless night, but there had been a sense of peace in her wakefulness. A peace she had long been seeking.

She had been planning the party for many months. Óttar was the love of her life – the man she wanted to spend the rest of her days with. He was popular, strong and influential. She had even announced to her friends that in him she had found an alpha male. He worked long hours, and was often a little preoccupied, but he could also be unbelievably charming. He brought her beautiful gifts, opened doors for her and sent flowers to her at work; just the way it should be. Her friends liked him – a lot; sometimes she even thought they were envious. This wasn't so much envy over him, as of their lifestyle. They weren't living together, but they spent every weekend in each other's company, normally in bed, when they weren't travelling the world. There wasn't a restaurant in the city where they hadn't eaten. There were invitations to every cultural event – to all the premieres and opening nights.

These last eighteen months had been a wonderful adventure. As the weeks passed, Erla found her love for Óttar deepen. She was now thirty-seven, and sensed that she was ready for something more. This was a new feeling. As a child she had looked forward to a family of her own: Mum, Dad, children. Then the longing had somehow passed, and Erla had enjoyed life to the full, working her dream job and being with her friends.

But something changed when Óttar came on the scene. Maybe it was a cliché – sometimes life *is* a cliché – but Erla began to feel a kind of fear of time, of how it flew by so quickly.

The day of Óttar's fiftieth had finally come. It was a beautiful Thursday in July and the weather couldn't have been more perfect. He thought he was on his way to a modest barbecue with his mother and his sister, and, of course, Erla. When she had met him the previous day he had suspected nothing, not a thing. She had told him to look forward to a cosy evening with the most important women in his life, and that he needed to be home by half past six. Nothing could be allowed to go wrong. Erla pulled herself out of bed and called the caterer to make sure everything was ready for tonight.

'I put the stack of pancakes on the table in the living room,' warbled Thrúður, Óttar's mother.

Thrúður had a slight figure. In certain respects she was like Erla, both of them of medium height, with narrow hips but broader across the shoulders and chest than most women. Erla's mother had told her that she should bear her shoulders with pride, as they showed that her ancestors had been women who had toiled tirelessly in the wild northern winds in order to keep their heads above water and their families alive.

'Hard-working women need space for their lungs,' she had said joyfully.

The memory brought a smile to Erla's lips.

Thrúður normally had her dark, grey-shot hair pulled into a neat ponytail at the back of her head, but on special occasions she would put it up in an immaculate bun. She used make-up sparingly, as she had a fairly dark complexion, although she always wore lipstick, alternating three colours, depending on the occasion. Today it was deep red. This meant the occasion was seriously important. For her only son's big birthday, anything less would be unthinkable.

Erla had brought in a caterer to provide the food. A delightful table had been set up, decorated with flower arrangements and bearing an elegant display of small dishes all on an American barbecue theme. He loved barbecue cuisine. A great deal of effort had gone into preparing the table and the food so that his favourite dishes were tastefully presented, but the guests didn't feel drenched in barbecue sauce or left the party with it on their fine clothing.

Erla had told his mother that she didn't need to do anything. All the same, Thrúður had arrived with a stack of rolled, sugared pancakes. Erla checked the table and noticed the pile sitting in its brown ovenproof bowl, sticking out of the tasteful table setting as if a tower block had been erected in the middle of the old city. She had placed it between the mini-burgers and the stylish plate of delicate mac and cheese dishes.

'Wonderful, thank you!' Erla said, giving Thrúður a smile that was entirely fake. She would ask the chef to re-arrange things later on, when Thrúður would be less likely to notice. She couldn't stand those bloody sugar-sweet pancakes of theirs.

She had noticed early on in their relationship that Óttar always made an effort to show his mother his best side. And she couldn't help finding this somehow fake, as if he were playing the role of the perfect, loving son. No one ever mentioned his father, who had left the country, abandoning his young family, and never returning. Or at least that was the story. Óttar had told her that Thrúður had searched for him for weeks, asking everyone they knew if they'd seen him, calling hotels around the world and weeping inconsolably.

Then, one morning he had woken up to find that everything had changed. His mother had been ready with porridge and sweet, sugared pancakes, immaculate and with a new smile on her lips. The appearance of that smile had been the moment when his father vanished from their lives. His name was never mentioned again. That smile remained with them to this day, and Erla noticed that Óttar frequently used the same smile himself in his dealings with his mother.

Óttar's sister Stefanía tapped at the door and came in.

'*Hæ!* Mum? Erla? Sorry I'm late. I thought I'd never get away. Work is just crazy right now. Everyone's making the most of the fine weather and they all want gardening advice.'

Thrúður glowed, telling her not to worry, that the chef had prepared everything, while she had made the sugared pancakes that she and her brother were so fond of, so everything was ready. Under other circumstances, Erla might have taken offence at Thrúður making no mention of all the efforts she had put into organising the party. But today Erla couldn't find it in herself to care.

The three of them, Thrúður, Stefania and Óttar, had a world of their own, each with a distinct role to play. The link between mother and daughter was straightforward: each enjoyed the support of the other and they were closer than many mother-daughter relationships Erla knew of. Óttar's connection with his sister, who was two years his elder, was similar to his relationship with his mother. It was as if Stefanía worried about him constantly, and felt she had to keep a watchful eye on him. Stefanía was something of a mystery to Erla. She lived alone and was at her best at the garden centre where she worked as a horticulturist. She was outstandingly attractive, with thick, dark hair that flowed halfway down her back, and almond-shaped green eyes. She was medium height but with a more delicate frame than her mother's. She preferred jeans and hoodies, but had made an effort today, with a pair of close-fitting, brightly coloured trousers and a white blouse that highlighted her elegant figure and natural beauty. Her nature was more relaxed than Óttar's or Thrúður's, and she laughed more easily. In this respect Erla envied her – Stefanía appeared to be completely satisfied with the little world she had created around her. She was also so positive, often fighting the corner of people she heard being talked down, pointing out that there was something good to be found in everyone. Erla felt that this was a wonderful quality.

It was almost six and the guests were starting to arrive. She had invited Óttar's colleagues from the ministry, his golfing buddies and some old friends. She had wanted to take him by surprise by inviting people he hadn't seen in years, but she'd had to search back a long way to track anyone down. It had turned out to be quite a challenge, as while everyone she spoke to remembered Óttar, she sensed that their connections with him lacked any real depth. Thrúður had made an attempt to dissuade her from searching too far back, encouraging her to stick with people he currently socialised with, but Erla hadn't let herself be told. Two of his old connections from the Commercial College had shown up. They arrived together and seemed unsure of why they had been invited. They stood by one window watching the rest of the gathering curiously, not mingling with the other guests. Under other circumstances Erla would have tried to engage them in conversation, to find out a little of what Óttar had been like as a younger man, but she somehow couldn't; instead she avoided their questioning gaze and looked away. She was beginning to feel some trepidation about this party. Perhaps it hadn't been a good idea to invite the old acquaintances along. Perhaps the whole party wasn't such a great plan after all. She wasn't feeling that positive about it now. It was a bit of a relief that Thrúður had now taken it upon herself to look after the caterers. Time crawled past, and Erla felt she was observing the guests through a mist as they waited with understated expectation for the birthday boy to make his appearance.

It turned six-thirty, but there was no sign of Óttar. Stefanía asked the ministry's permanent secretary if something at work had delayed her brother. The reply was that he hadn't seen him all day. In fact, nobody seemed to have seen him that day, although with so many people on holiday that wasn't particularly unusual.

Helgi, the permanent secretary, and Óttar were good friends. Helgi was a civil-service heavyweight, respected across political lines, as he had served professionally and conscientiously under ministers from almost every party. Óttar had mentioned to Erla that Helgi was preparing for retirement, and it seemed to Erla that Óttar was considering applying for the permanent secretary position. She had no doubt that the job would be his for the taking. He could twist anyone around his little finger.

The guests were now showing signs of becoming uneasy and impatient, which was understandable considering the enticing aroma of the food; but nobody had dared touch anything because the party couldn't start without the guest of honour. Stefanía had tried several times to call Óttar, but he still hadn't picked up.

Erla could feel the pitying eyes of the guests following her. Poor thing. She's made all this effort. Some of them had started on the champagne, having waited for half an hour for it. Her friend Guðrún came towards her with such a look of sympathy on her face that Erla decided to avoid speaking to her. She just couldn't bring herself to do it, so she scurried away and hid in the little bathroom next to Óttar's bedroom.

By nine o'clock, the guests had started to drift away. Guðrún offered to stay behind to help her clear up, but Erla forced a convincing smile onto her face and told her to go home, she'd call her in a day or two, promising every detail of the furious tirade Óttar would receive on his return home. Erla was still managing to hold it together when a group from the ministry, determined not to let the evening go to waste, crowded into taxis to take them to Andvari, the latest chic place to be.

Thrúður put away the pancakes, smiled awkwardly and began to make excuses for her son. 'He'll have been working, Erla my dear. You know what he's like.'

As soon as she was alone, Erla sat numbly on the sofa and looked at the exquisite American-style barbecue, which now looked like the forlorn mess it really was – crude outdoor food swimming in grease, dressed up as elegant French canapés. What had she been thinking? She gazed out of the window of Óttar's smart apartment in the downtown Shadow District, pulled her knees up under her chin and began to cry. How the hell had it come to this?

25.03.1995

I have butterflies in my stomach all day, every day. He wants to be with me all the time. Me!! I feel so good.

Mum is so happy I'm smiling more. So she's stopped smothering me with all her worries. And she's giving me more space too. Space to live my life and be with him. My Mr Sweet.

✳ 2 ✳

Garðar had become sick and tired of the pressure for yet more cost-cutting measures within the police force. What would they be asking him to do next? Sell off all the cars and say he could send his team to crime scenes on roller skates? Yesterday he had been reminded that at the current rate of spending, the year's financial resources would be gone by October. Another day of searching high and low for possible ways to make savings awaited him.

He had been on the force for a long time. He had joined as a young man and had worked his way up to head of CID at the city force. Sometimes he longed to quit, but couldn't see what job opportunities there might be for a man of his age, with only eight years to retirement.

Garðar was about to stand up to fetch the day's first cup of coffee when Unnar burst in.

'A man – a body – has been found on the beach,' he gasped, struggling for breath.

Garðar stood up now and came round his desk. 'Take a moment, Unnar, then tell me all the details.'

Unnar ran his hand through his hair and seemed to pull himself together. 'It's a beach east of Stokkseyri. Some Japanese tourists were taking a helicopter tour over the Eyjafjallajökull volcano, and on the way back they spotted the body, lying motionless on the beach. The pilot notified local police straight away. The local guys got to the scene about a quarter of an hour ago and they've just called for support from us. I've asked Viktor to have a car ready downstairs so we can get going immediately.'

Garðar put on his jacket and told Unnar to inform the forensic pathologist.

Flashing blue lights got them quickly through Reykjavík's heavy morning traffic and onto the main highway to Iceland's south coast. Once they were out of the city, the road quickly cleared and the majority of vehicles they encountered were buses and rental cars, driving slowly so the passengers could take in the landscape of lava fields and the natural steam dancing into the air from the geothermal power plant. The volume of tourist traffic had increased significantly in recent years and at this point in July there were holidaymakers everywhere. Garðar quietly approved of the growth in tourism – on a personal level at least. He felt the influx of travellers had brought new life to the country. He recalled when he had first got to know his wife, Gunnhildur, there had been just three good restaurants he could invite her to, and they had been ruinously expensive. Now there were great-quality restaurants and eateries on every corner and so far at least, the prices had remained acceptable.

They were just at the end of Threngslin pass when a report came through that an ambulance was at the scene as well as two patrol cars from the local force, plus one car that had been sent immediately from Reykjavík. The pathologist was also on the road not far behind them. Garðar hoped this would turn out to be a straightforward accident with a quick investigation. There were dozens of cases awaiting his department's attention, and the upcoming weekend would require a heavier police presence on the streets to keep the traffic flowing through the city and around it.

They pulled up where the first responders had parked their

vehicles, by the side of the road close to the beach. The area was a bit off the beaten track. The landscape was flat here, with fields behind them wearing their summer green, dressed up with yellow dots of buttercups.

As they made their way through the rocks to the location of the corpse, Garðar looked out at the sea. It was calm today, grey with a blueish tone, stretching out along the coastline, a few lonesome clouds forming images for the imagination to play with. The man lay on his back among the rocks along the shore. He was barefoot and soaked through, but Garðar saw nothing that might tell him how long he had been there. The coast between Eyrarbakki and Stokkseyri was popular with tourists, who frequently stopped to take pictures of the beach that stretched away as far as the eye could see – rocky but with areas of soft, beautiful sand, which was golden-brown and sometimes black. Garðar recalled childhood visits to this coastline with his father. He had always made time for him as a boy and taken him on numerous trips around the country. Garðar remembered him pointing to the sea one time they were here, and telling him that if he were to sail straight south, there would be no landfall until Antarctica. He was fond of this memory.

The officers who'd been first at the scene reported that they had not touched the body, deciding to wait for CID to arrive from Reykjavík.

'We don't reckon this is a tourist because we don't see a lot of people in suits around here,' said one, pointing to the smart clothes the man was wearing. 'Also, tourists don't often come this way. They normally stop to take their pictures more to the west of the town, closer to Eyrarbakki.'

Garðar couldn't make out the man's face, as his head was turned away from them. He saw dark hair and a soaked shirt, its sleeves rolled up. The man's jacket lay, carefully folded, further up the beach.

Unnar had begun to photograph the body and the scene around it, when he lowered the camera and called to Garðar that there was something familiar about the man.

'Any idea who he is?' Garðar called back.

'I can't be sure, but I'm sure I've seen him before.'

Garðar picked his way through the rocks and bent over so he could see the man's face.

He straightened up in surprise.

He'd recognised Óttar Karlsson immediately. Óttar, otherwise referred to as The Panther, worked at the Ministry of Finance, where he managed the department responsible for state property. They had met a few times recently, as Óttar was preparing the sale of the police headquarters in the centre of Reykjavík to some foreign hotel chain. He was a good-looking, charming man, with a reputation for getting his own way.

'Looks like an accident, don't you think?' Unnar muttered as he took more pictures.

'Never make assumptions,' Garðar said as he scanned the scene and Óttar's lifeless body. 'Let's wait and see what the pathologist has to say ... and I see he's just arrived.'

✳ 3 ✳

SIGURDÍS

I'm snatched from sleep by the sound of something crashing to the floor upstairs. This old house is built of wood so it feels like the ceiling is about to come down on me. I leap out of bed and stand, confused, in the middle of the floor, rubbing my eyes. Then I hear the crashing noise again. This isn't the first time he's woken me up like this. It's happened for as long as I remember. The bastard.

I tiptoe up the stairs. There's a tight knot of fear in my gut. My stone. I must have been born with it, as I don't remember ever not having this stone in my belly. On rare occasions, this familiar companion gives me courage and energy – it seems to flare up like a fireball, sending streams of energy into my limbs. But normally it doesn't. It just feels like a big grey stone, weighing me down, leaving me crippled with fear. Right now, I can feel the anger and tension building up into a chaotic emotion – I'm waiting to see what awaits me this time around. Maybe Mum has finally knocked him out cold. I hope so. I can't face going up there to see Mum's face swollen with tears yet again, as she forces a smile and tells me to just go back downstairs and back to sleep. Does she really think I could do that? This is a fucking wooden house we live in! Why doesn't she just take us with her and run for it? Escape from this place and start over again without him.

They aren't in the passage upstairs. But then, making my way slowly into the living room, I hear Mum fall. I hear the piercing screech of the dining table shoved across the floor as Mum is hurled against it. These sounds are all so familiar. In the dining room I see Mum curled into a ball at the foot of the table, her face puffed with tears and bruises. The bastard's standing over her, yelling.

'Yeah, try and hide yourself away, you bitch. You're a stupid slag and a waste of fucking space!'

His curses seem to spur his anger still further, and he grabs at Mum, hauling her from under the table. Mum sees me and tries to stand up. His back is still turned to me as he punches her in the stomach with all the strength he has.

I can't stop myself. I run and leap onto his back, left hand over his eyes, hammering at him as hard as I can with my right. In his surprise and fury he shakes me off, throwing me against the wall behind him, where I collapse into a heap on the floor.

'Stop! Dad, stop!' yells my little brother from the doorway. Tiny and clad in smiley-face pyjamas, he throws himself at our father, who snarls that our mother is out of her mind and he has to keep her in order. He's just defending himself. When my brother won't let up, he changes his tune and yells:

'You two are just the same. Little shits!'

I've had enough. I'm going to leave. I'll take my little brother and leave this house. I try to stand up, but my left leg won't respond. It must be broken. I watch helplessly as he rips my little brother off him. The little body is like a leaf in his hands. He slams him down, and his little head catches the edge of the table.

'Einar...' I howl, and I can hear the terror in my own voice. 'Einar!'

That's when I see the blood dripping from his head and pooling on the floorboards, seeping towards me. The pain in my leg vanishes from the shock, and I rush over to him. He won't wake up. He won't wake up!

'You've killed him, you bastard. Your own son!' I scream at my father.

Mum stands there in a daze for a second, then collapses onto the sofa.

'Mum,' I say, 'you let him kill your son!'

Dad leaves the room, and a moment later I hear the front door slam shut behind him.

✳ 4 ✳

'Last year I went with some girlfriends to stay in a summer cottage. Their idea was that we should all go on a juice fast, and the best way to make it work would be for all of us to go to Dóra's parents' place to relax and support each other, and that would be part of the cure. I woke up that first morning at around six and went outside to sit on a lovely bench that Dóra's parents had put next to the gravel path. Across the path was a patch of grass that had been left to itself for a long time. It was all dandelions, and weeds that a city kid like me wouldn't know the name of, although I do know a manicured lawn isn't for me. As I watched the grass waving in the wind and the insects buzzing around, I fell into some sort of trance, and it felt as if the world slowed right down. That was the first time I saw a horsefly in the wild. It was there among the dandelions, and I realised that this had to be its natural environment, and not against the shadowy walls of buildings, which were the only places I'd seen them before. I had often wondered what the link was between horseflies and walls. I could never figure out the point of them living their lives buzzing up and down walls.'

This was Sigurdís's last session with Thorgeir, the psychologist. She liked him. He applied no pressure, gave her all the time she needed and wasn't unnerved by long silences, which was a relief. But he was so close to the image she had formed of what a psychologist should look like that it was almost funny. He was slim, his back slightly hunched, he had a beard streaked with grey, and generally wore cord trousers, checked shirts and a dark-blue sweater. The final detail was how he would occasionally look at her over the top of his glasses. She really was starting to feel fond of him.

'What is it about horseflies that sparks your interest, Sigurdís?'

She had been sent to see him after jumping on a young man who had lashed out at his girlfriend in the city centre one night a year and a half ago. Sigurdís's recollection was that she had been unable to let the man go as she held him in a neck lock with one arm, punching him repeatedly and with all her strength with her free hand. The world around her had gone dark, while she yelled at the girlfriend to run for it. Sigurdís's fellow officer had finally managed to release her grip on the man, who had been left badly bruised. Her superiors had decided to send her to a psychologist and confined her to desk duty. Maybe they had too much sympathy for her to go as far as dismissing her, but more than likely they were still plagued with too much guilt on her account.

'Sometimes I feel like a horsefly on a wall. Lonely in a crowd and a little out of place.'

'Is that how you feel now?' Thorgeir asked, peering amiably at her over the top of the glasses perched slightly askew on his nose.

Sigurdís decided that a cheerful response would be in order, so he wouldn't have doubts about signing her off.

'No, not anymore. Or at any rate, not so often.'

This wasn't true, as this was how she felt most of the time. She appreciated the sessions with Thorgeir and had gone into them with an open mind, fully aware that she was carrying around a weight of emotional baggage she was struggling to cope with. But, although these sessions had been a great help to her, she doubted her wounds would ever heal completely. She had somehow accepted that was the way it was going to be, and decided that her only way through was to stand up straight and keep going, no matter what.

She frequently wondered whether Einar would have jumped onto their father's back if he hadn't seen her hang from his back first, then be thrown off, her leg broken in the fall. She and Einar had been close, and she made a habit of looking out for him. Had he felt that he owed it to her to go to her aid? If only she hadn't tried to be a hero ... If, if, if. All these 'ifs' were enough to drive anyone mad.

Sigurdís knew all this perfectly well, and was completely aware that she bore no blame for any of it, yet she was still unable to free herself from endlessly going over it in her mind. Einar had looked up to his big sister and she knew that he relied on her. He had never before taken the initiative like that. Generally he had tiptoed along in his sister's shadow, whether outdoors, or in her room, where she sang for him or told him stories until he fell asleep.

Thorgeir had reminded her that, like Einar, she had been a child, even though she had been fifteen. She had been a child who had no influence on that night's sequence of events. Sigurdís was fully aware of this, of course, but when her friends or Halla reminded her of the fact, she always retorted cheerfully that it was wrong to waste a perfectly good guilt complex.

The truth was she simply found it too difficult to stifle those thoughts that sought constantly to return to that evening, even though fourteen years had passed. Einar had survived, although his skull had been fractured and he had been kept in a coma for six weeks. This was something she would never be able to forget. She had promised herself that if he were to wake up and get to live, she would make sure that their bastard father never came near them again and she would make it all up to her brother. She was determined to ensure that he'd have security and love for the rest of his life. And she couldn't trust their mother to do that.

Sigurdís had so far kept her promise, and had been staunchly supported by Halla, their mother's sister – their wonderful Halla.

Their father had been arrested and sentenced to four years for assault and attempted manslaughter. On his release, he left the country, which was hardly a surprise as nobody was inclined to forgive him seventeen years of domestic violence that had culminated in the near-death of his son. And he knew that.

Their mother had suffered a breakdown and was admitted to a psychiatric ward, returning there regularly over the years that had elapsed since that night. It had fallen to Sigurdís and Halla to sit at Einar's bedside. Initially, Sigurdís refused to leave him, dozing at his bedside for ten days, with one leg in plaster, until her childhood friend Dóra's mother had managed to persuade her to come home with them, where she stayed for six months.

She had been furious with her mother for not getting help, for not leaving their father or doing anything, just anything, that could have prevented the violence. But her mother had been caught in the headlights. She and Sigurdís had barely had a conversation since, simply exchanging occasional platitudes. Her mother had told her – and it was true – that their father had never before laid a hand on his children.

'But he beat you black and blue, so it was only a question of when,' Sigurdís had shouted, slamming the door behind her.

When Einar came to and was ready for rehabilitation therapy, he and Sigurdís went to live with Halla. Their mother never recovered her health properly and felt it was best for them to be with her sister, who soon became their surrogate mother. Halla was eaten up with self-reproach for not having made more of an effort to get her sister out of the abusive marriage. Having initially been sure that things weren't that bad, she had only gradually come to realise the severity of the situation, her sister had been so skilled at hiding the reality, presenting a smile to the outside world. However, by the time she was pregnant with her son, the signs of abuse had become more visible. In addition to her own guilt, Halla was unhappy with a number of other individuals who could also have taken action earlier. Like Sigurdís, she suffered from a persistent *if*-complex. If she'd persisted, not let herself be fobbed off, maybe things would have been different.

As Sigurdís was leaving the therapist's office, her phone rang, and she saw it was Dóra calling.

'How did it go with Thorgeir, darling? Was he happy to sign you off?'

Sigurdís replied that everything had worked out perfectly and that this particular bruiser had been signed off for good.

'Don't talk about yourself like that,' said Dóra. 'You're a wonderful person who was born into horrific circumstances. It's no wonder you behave like that sometimes. Everything you went through has been heavy on your soul. Shall we meet up tonight? I'm going crazy at work and could do with a chat.'

Sigurdís agreed and said she would call her later in the day.

Ever since they had been small, Dóra had been her rock. The way things had been at home meant that Sigurdís always sought to be elsewhere. Fortunately, she had been the lively, impulsive type and had made many friends and looked for opportunities to eat and stay anywhere other than at her own home. She hated the sound of her mother weeping. She hated the sight of the false smile she forced on her face when Sigurdís asked why she didn't leave him. And she hated being anywhere near him. The more she avoided her own home, the more she came to understand that there was something very wrong with it. In other people's houses it was possible to watch the television together and laugh with no concern about what could happen later in the evening.

In other homes the dads took part in household tasks. They even did the dishes and hugged their wives affectionately. This was something she never saw, except when a show was put on for the rare visitors who called on them. The situation had started to worsen when her mother fell pregnant with Einar, and after his birth it had become unbearable.

Sigurdís's classmates set up a system to check on her after Einar was taken to hospital. They sat with her, made sure she ate and let her cry on their shoulders. They made sure that she stayed sane. Dóra's mother had been the one to go with her to court to give evidence against her father. After he had been sentenced, she had taken them out for a burger and a movie to cheer her up.

Sigurdís sometimes had the feeling that the system among her friends to keep her on track was still in use. It got on her nerves sometimes, although she was also grateful for it. Her friends didn't need to do any of this, could have just shied away from the girl who was nothing but trouble, but they hadn't – because they were genuinely fond of her and their behaviour showed that. She loved these girls and knew that what they had been through meant that the bonds would last her whole life through.

This would be the last day she would turn up late for work after a session with Thorgeir, and she was looking forward to normality.

I hope one day they'll stop treating me like a porcelain doll, Sigurdís thought.

After that altercation downtown, her younger colleagues had got to hear from her older colleagues the story of her past, and how her father – the police inspector himself, back then – had beaten his wife and daughter, and come close to killing his own son. It had subsequently gone around the station that her pent-up anger towards her father had boiled over, and had been directed at that young man. Sigurdís had often chuckled to herself at this TV-style psychology, feeling as if she were on Dr Phil's couch.

The leery boyfriend had been let off without charge – as had she. More than likely, everyone was happy, with the probable exception of the young man's girlfriend. Sigurdís hoped that she had given him the push, but felt it unlikely.

There was one thing that her father's old colleagues forgot to mention to their younger workmates when her problems were being analysed in the police canteen. This was that Halla had approached her father's fellow officers when her mother was pregnant with Einar, and told them that she thought he could be beating his wife. None of them had done anything – not a single thing.

Sigurdís arrived at the Hverfisgata station expecting a day of paperwork with Garðar. She had been told that she wasn't ready to go back to routine shifts.

'This is so not what I signed up for,' she had said to Garðar with a sigh the day before, when they had been filing away folders at the end of the day. He had looked at her with that paternal expression on his face, as if to say, *I know what's best for you*, and told her to go home early and take it easy. The subtext was she should enjoy being young and do something fun. And Sigurdís couldn't shake off the feeling that they still saw her as a rookie, even though she had been taking shifts since she had been twenty-one, and that made eight years.

Garðar and the others had kept an eye on her and Einar over the years, and after she finished college, he had given her some summer shifts. It had never been Sigurdís's intention to become a police officer, but that summer she felt the desire to do something useful, to help people – women and children – through police work. It was more than likely that behind this desire there was also a need to make sense of why none of the bastard's colleagues had done anything after Halla's warning that he was beating his wife. She had to ensure that nothing like this could happen again.

So, she had given up on her history degree and enrolled in the police college two years after her first summer relief shift. And she'd done well. She had been on the beat ever since, right up until that night when she had so memorably lost it. Sigurdís told herself that there was no need to beat herself up over it, as the idiot boy had had it coming, but she was also keenly aware that if she wanted to make a difference, and put idiots like him behind bars, then she would have to follow the rules.

That was why she had attended sessions with Thorgeir so willingly, and with an open mind, so she would get the help she needed to maintain control under such circumstances. Deep down, she also longed to be free of the stone in her belly, and the loneliness she so often felt. She had no desire to live her life like a horsefly knocking against a shadowy wall.

* 5 *

'Where's Garðar?' Sigurdís asked Viktor when she reached the office.

Viktor, one of the younger detectives, was sitting at his desk, looking lost, as if he didn't know what to do next.

'They went out to Stokkseyri,' he said. 'A body's been found on the beach there.'

'When was this?' Sigurdís walked over to Viktor and stood in front of him. She couldn't help feeling it was typical that a big, important case should come in while she was off duty. 'Give me the details.'

All Viktor knew was that the team had been at the location for a couple of hours and they were checking the whole area. Sigurdís called Garðar's cellphone. He wasn't picking up, so she went over to her computer and checked through the news media. Various sites were already carrying reports of the body on the beach, and journalists and photographers had clearly made it to the scene, as grainy images, obviously taken from a distance, had been put online. Nobody was being allowed too close, of course, so the pictures were all of the rocky shoreline and the team working around what must be the body.

Her phone began to buzz. Garðar was calling back.

'Why didn't you call me? I'd have come with you,' Sigurdís said, without bothering with a greeting.

'We had to leave in a hurry this morning, so I thought I'd leave you to have your appointment with Thorgeir,' Garðar replied. 'But we'll be back soon. The whole area has been photo-graphed and the pathology team is finishing their stuff so that the body can be moved. Any traces of evidence are going to be difficult to find though,' he continued thoughtfully. 'The ocean tides round here are so strong, they'll have washed much of it away, unfortunately. At least the body was high enough up the beach that the tide didn't carry it out to sea.'

'So it's a man? Any idea who he is?' Sigurdís asked, as she continued to scan the online news.

'Yes. That's what's interesting. He's a senior civil servant at the Ministry of Finance, but some years back he was a prominent figure in politics. But let's keep this to ourselves until I get back. We're going to have to be quick about informing the family before the media sniff out who he is.'

'Was this an accident, Garðar?'

'I'm afraid not, considering the state of him. But we'll have to wait for the autopsy results before we can confirm anything. Can you call the whole team in and tell them to meet us at three-thirty in the meeting room on the third floor? We'll set up an incident room there and the team will work on this from there. Could you sort that out for me? If it turns out it was an accident after all, then we'll just have to clear the meeting room out again.'

'Of course,' Sigurdís said, and ended the call.

She walked over to Viktor's desk. She'd need his help to set up everything that was needed.

'We'll need a computer for the big screen, and we'll need to collect more monitors from the other rooms and hook them up to computers.'

'Don't we need an ordinary board as well, for the dinosaurs?' Viktor said with a grin.

'Good idea. Two whiteboards as well. We need to organise the tables into work units: one for analysing his life – family, friends, colleagues, daily life, past and so on; another one for the data from the scene and the pathology information; and a third for Garðar and case management, to go through all the information and take decisions on what comes next.'

'Wow. You're properly on the ball today, Sigurdís.'

'This is basic stuff, isn't it?' she replied. If she couldn't be at the crime scene, at least she was able to organise things. She'd come up with this layout on the spur of the moment, and she hoped her instincts weren't too far off the mark and Garðar would think the room was ready for what lay ahead.

Garðar started the session by going through the information that was already available.

'Pathology's opinion, based on what they saw at the scene, is that this is unlikely to have been an accident, but we can't rule that out until we have the autopsy findings. He's most likely to have been on the beach since Wednesday evening or the early hours of Thursday. So, at least twenty-four hours. Pathology should be able to give us a more accurate time of death soon, and we should have a cause of death later today. We need to split up into teams right away, as we're working on the assumption that this is a murder investigation. To start with, we need to meet his family and inform them. We'll have to be quick, as the press will try everything to find out the identity of the deceased. There are hacks who have already tracked down the helicopter company and they've spoken to the tourists who noticed the body.'

'I'll find out who his next of kin are,' Sigurdís said.

'Unnar, I want you on this as well,' Garðar said. 'But I reckon it's best if Sigurdís and I deal with the relatives together. Considering who the deceased is, I ought to be the one to deliver the news, but it always helps to have a female officer as well.'

Sigurdís decided not to allow this to irritate her, even though she hated being assigned this or that role simply because she was a woman. She knew what it meant though. The shoulder Garðar would offer the relatives to cry on would be hers, and he would get away without having to provide any solace.

At least I'm part of the team on this, Sigurdís thought to herself. If this did turn out to be a murder, it would be the first time she was involved in a major investigation.

6

Óttar Karlsson's mother lived in a small, terraced house on Ásgarður, part of a neighbourhood built in the early sixties in an effort to provide affordable housing for low-income families. After the Second World War, Reykjavík grew fast and soon found itself in the midst of a housing crisis, with many poorer families having to live in army barracks in the camps the British and later the Americans had left behind. Before Garðar was born his parents had lived in one of these barracks with his two older siblings, after moving to the city from the countryside of northern Iceland. They had told him stories about life in the old army camps – the dampness and cold air, but also the colourful characters they had met. When the city council started offering low-income families new housing opportunities, Garðar's family had been one of the first to escape the poor living conditions in the barracks. By the time Garðar was born, their standard of living had improved, so he only knew what a struggle their life had been from the tales he'd been told.

Sigurdís and Garðar had decided to change into civil clothing and drive in an unmarked car, so as to not alarm the elderly lady or pique the neighbours' curiosity. They parked a little way from the house, outside the neighbourhood church, and walked the rest of the way. The home was immaculate, with a neat display of flowers in an elegant pot by the door and a crafted wooden bench on which lay an ashtray, which sparkled as if it had never been used.

Sigurdís rang the doorbell, and the initial response was the barks from the dog next door. Garðar was preoccupied, wondering how to break the news to this woman of her son's death. Sigurdís had no idea how to break news like this to a victim's close family. Her stomach ached with trepidation and her palms were clammy with sweat.

'Thrúður Karlsdóttir?'

Óttar's mother had obviously not been expecting visitors and opened the door no more than halfway.

She was a good-looking woman, around seventy but young for her age, with dark hair turning grey, pinned up with a clip. She wore grey slippers and a grey dressing gown that she held tight around her as she looked them up and down.

'Yes, that's me,' she said. Then nodded to her attire. 'I'm sorry, but I wasn't expecting anyone. I don't often get visitors these days.'

Garðar cleared his throat. 'My name is Garðar Sigurgeirsson and this is Sigurdís Hölludóttir. We are from the city police CID.'

Thrúður looked surprise. 'Have the boys in the house at the end of the terrace been stealing bicycles again?' she asked with a sigh.

'Unfortunately it's nothing so trivial. Could we come inside?'

The smell of disinfectant hit their noses as they entered. The house was pristine, everything in its place – it was as if the place was barely occupied. The furniture was sparse and minimalist in shades of teak and grey. Thrúður invited them to take a seat on the sofa in the little living room then looked at them curiously.

'I'll get straight to the point,' Garðar said. 'I'm sorry to tell you that your son Óttar was found dead this morning. Some Japanese tourists on a sightseeing flight saw him lying on the beach east of Stokkseyri. All the indications are that he died on Wednesday night or in the early hours of Thursday.'

Thrúður said nothing. She sat rigidly and stared into space.

'Our deepest condolences. We have already informed the local priest and he will be visiting you this afternoon. Is there anyone else we should inform?'

Thrúður said nothing. Garðar and Sigurdís exchanged glances, tacitly agreeing to give her some time to absorb the news. After what seemed to Sigurdís to be an age, Thrúður stood up and asked if they would like some water, before going to the kitchen. After a moment, they heard the tap turning on and the sound of running water. It was allowed to flow for a very long time.

Finally, Sigurdís decided to go into the kitchen, and found Thrúður sitting on the floor, her back to the sink. She was rigid. Sigurdís turned off the water and sat on the floor at the woman's side. She could see tears running down the woman's face.

Thrúður turned slightly and looked at her. 'He was doing so well. I thought he must have been cheating on Erla, or they had had some disagreement, and that's why he didn't turn up yesterday for his birthday party. My son was fifty yesterday, you see. Did you know that? ... How could this happen? What was he doing all the way out there? What happened to him?'

Sigurdís took her hand as Garðar appeared in the kitchen.

'We don't know exactly what happened,' he said. 'He has injuries to his head and face, as well as some bruising, and one shin bone is broken. The pathologists are working to determine the cause of death and we're waiting for their conclusions. Can we call anyone for you?'

'What about Óttar's father – Karl?' Sigurdís asked.

Thrúður looked into her eyes, her gaze sharper now. 'He walked out when the children were small and we haven't heard a word from him since. And his name's not Karl. That slob's name is Ómar Albertsson. After he left, I didn't want my children carrying his name, so they took my father's instead as their patronymic.'

'You have a daughter, don't you?' Sigurdís said. 'Can we call her?'

'No. I'll do it myself,' Thrúður said.

She closed her eyes, and seemed to be drawing some kind of strength from somewhere Then she got to her feet and went over to where her bag lay on the kitchen counter.

She took out her phone and called, her face blank and tight. When her daughter answered, Thrúður simply announced: 'Óttar is dead, Stefanía. Can you come? The police are here.' And then she ended the call. She appeared not to have waited for any response from her daughter. Most likely she had been unable to cope with saying anything more.

Sigurdís wondered about the unfortunate Stefanía. What was it like to receive such a call from your mother without any further explanation, and then for the line to go dead? She saw the phone on the counter light up as Stefanía tried to call back.

'I'm not answering. She'll come,' Thrúður said in a flat voice.

'Would you like us to wait for her to arrive?' Sigurdís asked.

Thrúður shook her head. 'When should I expect the priest? Stefanía and I will talk to him about ... about all this,' she said in the same level tone.

'He should be here shortly. If you have any questions, then please feel free to call at any time, day or night,' Garðar said, handing her a card. 'We'll be in touch when we have more information on the cause of death.'

They were by the open front door when something Thrúður said came back to Sigurdís. 'You mention someone called Erla. Who is she?'

'Óttar's long-term girlfriend. They've been a couple for a while but don't live together. I had been hoping Óttar would marry this one and make me a grandmother.' Thrúður looked through the open door into the distance. 'But she's as career-minded as he is, so they would probably have never found the time...'

✳ 7 ✳

THRÚÐUR

It's three years today since Ómar left. It's a relief – and it isn't. I don't understand what happened. We maybe weren't the world's happiest couple, but we lived a pretty good life together. We had lovely children and a flat in Hafnarfjörður, so we were secure. He always came straight home after work. I put dinner on the table and we'd sit and talk about the day with the children. He was often distant, but it never crossed my mind that he could just vanish. We had practically given up on sex, though. He didn't seem to have an appetite for it, or maybe just not with me. He did have a nasty side, but generally he sat quietly in front of the TV or over a book.

I couldn't bring myself to go to work this morning. I put on a brave face for the children before they went to school, but sometimes I need to be alone and a sick day comes in useful. Working as a nursing assistant is also physically demanding. My doctor wants me to get checked for arthritis. I'm not having that. Most likely it's just inflamed muscles, fatigue and maybe a bit of depression. There can't be anything else wrong with me. I've no intention of being branded an invalid when there are probably straightforward explanations. And, of course, I also need to provide for all of us.

This film is terribly dull. I've never been one for movies like this, but this one is extraordinarily bad. Dúa turned up with a video tape and said I had to watch it, said she couldn't get it out of her mind after seeing it. Well, maybe that's because it's so boring! *Gone with the Wind* – what a load of rubbish: spoilt brats treating other people – their slaves – badly. They pretend they're such fine folk, and then never pay them a penny for all that servitude. That's the way the world still is. It's full of spoilt brats and people who slave from morning to night. My children aren't going to be someone's slaves. I'll make sure they learn that.

Ach, I can't be having with answering the door now. It'll only be some young men in smart coats wanting to tell you about their faith. It's so damned rude, ringing time and again. I'll give them a peace of my mind this time.

'What's the matter with you people?' I shout from my chair. 'Can't I get a little peace and quiet?'

'Thrúður, it's Dúa. I saw your car outside. Are you going to let me in?'

'Sorry, sorry … Yes, of course.'

So much for peace and quiet. There goes my day of recharging my batteries so I can keep pretending that everything's just fine.

'Is something up?' I ask, opening the door.

'No, I just called the hospital and they said you were ill, so I thought I'd stop by. I wanted a word face to face. Gúna, Daði's mother, wanted a couple of us mums to have a chat together yesterday.'

'Really? Is there something going on at the school, or between the boys?'

'I don't quite know where to start.'

'What's going on? And why wasn't I asked to join this chat? Am I that useless and boring, or do they just think I'm not important enough to be included?'

Dúa walks in without being invited and goes straight into my kitchen and sits at the table. Her eyes are downcast as she thinks what to say.

Finally she looks up at me. 'We got together to discuss Óttar's behaviour towards the boys in the neighbourhood.'

I pause a moment. Then say, 'All right. Well, if he's being rude, or he's teasing someone, then I'll have a word and make sure he leaves them alone.'

'It's more than that.' Dúa shakes her head. 'Daði broke down a few days ago and told his older brother that he had killed a cat. He put it in a thick plastic bag and taped it shut so that it suffocated. He hasn't been back to school because he's been so upset.'

'And what does this have to do with Óttar?'

'Daði says that it was Óttar's idea, and that he held him down while the cat was fighting to get out of the bag, stopped him from opening it and letting it go. When the cat stopped moving, Óttar laughed and called Daði a softie, that it was just a stupid cat that didn't matter.'

I don't know what to say to this. I take a deep breath to dislodge the sob that's caught in my throat. I consider sitting down, but instead I lean back against the sink and look down at the patterned lino on the floor. Dúa gets up from the kitchen table and comes over to me. I feel sick at the thought of her coming close to me. I don't want that. What was I thinking, leaning up against the sink in this tiny kitchen? I can't easily get past her and out of here. I have to stand straight, look her in the eye.

'I know this must be difficult to hear, Thrúður. I'm so sorry to be the one to tell you all this. You have enough problems already, but you're my friend and I want you to know what's being said. You remember last summer, when Agga's little boy was found in the brook, barely alive? He recovered, thankfully, but it could easily have been so much worse. He hasn't been outside to play or walked on his own to school since, and nobody could figure out why. Now he's told his parents that

Óttar had been tormenting him, that he held him down in the brook until he couldn't remember anything more. He hadn't wanted to say anything, because he was frightened of Óttar.'

I grip the edge of the sink tightly. The metal is cold against my hands. 'What the hell are you saying? Are the neighbourhood mums getting together in the evenings to organise a witch-hunt of a ten-year-old boy? How on earth can you think that my child would do anything like that? He might be a bit wild sometimes, but he's done so well since his father left. Is the whole neighbourhood talking like this about him?' I'm trembling now.

'Not the whole neighbourhood, no.' Dúa is trying to soften her voice, but I can see there's more to come. 'There are other rumours are going around though. He seems to have Daði completely under his thumb – Daði does everything Óttar tells him, because he says Óttar is his friend and looks after him. You'll have seen how socially awkward Daði is, so he was delighted that he finally had a friend. But after the story about the cat came out, Daði was in floods of tears and told his mother something else...' She has to look away from me now. 'He told her Óttar made him put his hand inside a little girl's knickers while Óttar held her down.'

'Dúa, stop it,' I say. I want to push past her, but she's standing so close, I feel trapped. I can't help but go on the attack. 'Does it never occur to these old gossips that their own kids might be lying little bastards? And in Óttar they just found an easy target? I don't believe a word of it and I won't have you talking about him like that!'

I have to make every effort not to cry. She can't see me in tears. I need to get this woman out of here. I'm sure I'm seeing double and my head starts to spin. And it's like I don't recognise Dúa; it's as if there's a complete stranger in front of me and her voice seems to echo around the room.

'It's best that you go.'

'Are you sure you want to be alone?'

'Yes.'

'Thrúður, I have to tell you one more thing. This could become an official matter. Agga is thinking about taking it to the police. And so is the mother of another boy who was also put in the brook—'

'I want you to go now,' I interrupt before she can say anything else. 'I have nothing more to say except that you need not be concerned about my son in future.'

My son will do well for himself. I'll make sure of that. We'll show these old gossips what we're made of.

* 8 *

Erla was a good-looking woman, and Sigurdís noticed that she also looked physically fit, someone who clearly took care of herself. Dark hair fell in waves over her slim shoulders. She had beautiful grey eyes, ringed with black eyeliner. Sigurdís imagined they would usually be sparkling, but today they looked sadly blank – the eyes of a woman in sorrow and shock.

Garðar introduced himself and Sigurdís, before offering their condolences and their apologies for intruding on such a painful moment. 'I'm afraid Óttar's death is being investigated as a murder,' he went on, 'so we have to speak to everyone as soon as possible, as part of our investigation.'

Erla's tasteful apartment was in one of the grand old apartment buildings in the west of Reykjavík. Erla's apartment was on the main floor, and beautiful broad steps, with carved cement handrails on both sides, led up to the front door. Erla showed them in, and Sigurdís noticed that clothes were scattered around the apartment, and that pictures plucked from albums had been spread out over a table in the living room. These were both recent and older pictures. Some were of Óttar and Erla, and others were of two little girls. Sigurdís's eyes wandered to one photo of the two little girls, each in what seemed to be her mother's arms, dressed in eighties outfits, or so Sigurdís guessed. It was a bright, happy scene, and had been taken in front of a building that looked familiar, but Sigurdís could not place.

Erla was wearing fashionable beige pyjamas and carried

herself like a ballerina. She wore no make-up, and it was obvious that she had been crying. She coughed and gestured towards the sofa, inviting them to sit down. Then she apologised for the mess and began picking up the pictures with trembling hands, before disappearing with a stack of them into the bedroom.

'Would you like coffee?' she asked as she returned, but they declined. So she sat down opposite them and offered a strained smile.

Garðar led the questioning, and encouraged Erla to tell them about the events of the last couple of days. She told them about the surprise birthday party she had planned, and how Óttar had failed to turn up to it. Hadn't even called. And she confirmed that the last contact she'd had with him had been on Wednesday evening, two days ago now, when she had spoken to him and led him to believe there would be just a small gathering around the barbecue the following day for his fiftieth birthday. Garðar asked her to tell them a bit about her relationship with Óttar, and her face crumpled. He had been the love of her life, she told them, and now she felt like she'd been completely cast adrift. Then she burst into tears, unable to hold them back anymore.

'Is there anyone who comes to mind who could have wanted to do him harm?' Garðar asked when the tears had subsided.

'No, but I don't know a lot about what goes on in his work life. I did notice that there were people who sometimes called him at weekends or in the evenings, and some of them clearly weren't happy. But we had an agreement to not talk any more than necessary about work while we were together. We just wanted to relax and enjoy life. We're good at that,' Erla said, and the tears erupted again. 'We *were* good at that. I guess I'm going to have to get used to saying "we were" from now on.' She dabbed at the tears with the sleeve of her pyjama top. 'Anyway, I didn't make a habit of telling him about my work either. I'm a lawyer, and that's mostly the kind of work best left at the office.

You'd go mad if you didn't. So we liked to have our separate existence – just the two of us and no interruptions.' She stared into space now. 'But you see where that led,' she said in a low, flat voice. 'I can't even tell you what he was busy with at work, or who called him when we were at home.'

Looking around, as Erla spoke, Sigurdís saw framed pictures on the walls of people from various time periods. She noticed a hook where one picture seemed to be missing, and it occurred to her that this might have been one of Óttar that Erla couldn't bear to have in view.

'Do you have any leads?' Erla was on her feet now, fidgeting with the string of her pyjamas, her eyes shifting from one of them to the other.

'Unfortunately not,' Garðar said. 'So far all we can tell you is that he lost his life late on Wednesday evening due to a heavy blow to the head. This wasn't immediately fatal, and he may have lain there for some time before being overcome by his injuries. We found his jacket and shoes close by, but there's no sign of his phone. Do you know what type of phone he had?'

'Some kind of Samsung that the Ministry provided. He always had it with him, so it's strange if it wasn't on him. Could someone have taken it? The person who did this to him?'

'We don't know at this point,' Garðar replied.

'Can you tell us a bit about Óttar's friends?' Sigurdís asked. 'Is there someone we could talk to about him that might be able to help?' She judged this was the right kind of question to ask at this point, but still glanced at Garðar to see his reaction.

'He didn't have many friends,' said Erla, sitting down again. 'But he did have a very large circle of acquaintances. When I was organising his birthday party and tried to find some childhood friends from his high school and college years, I did think it was odd that it was so difficult to track anyone down. And I couldn't find anyone who had been at primary school with him. He always said he hadn't maintained contact with anyone from those days, though, and Thrúður said she couldn't think of anyone in particular to invite. I finally found a few people who were at the Commercial College with him, and two of them turned up, although I didn't get the feeling that they had been in any way his close friends. Maybe they went out on the lash now and again, but nothing more than that.'

'And his friends from university?'

'He studied engineering in America, so I wouldn't know about them. I can't think of anyone he has stayed in touch with.'

'Where did he study in America?'

'The University of Minnesota. A really good university. I'm surprised Thrúður didn't tell you about that. She's so proud of him, she announces it to anyone within earshot.'

'She hasn't been able to say much since we informed her of Óttar's death,' Sigurdís said.

'She worshipped him.' Erla let out a long sigh and stared at the wall ahead of her. 'At any rate, she called all the time and they had a conversation every evening about what kind of a day he'd had. She must be devastated.' She looked back at Garðar. 'Have you spoken to Stefanía, his sister?'

'Only briefly. She's in shock and hasn't been able to say much either,' Garðar said. 'Now, would you mind if we had a look around the flat? Sometimes it can help us...'

Erla nodded and flapped a hand to show they could do what they wanted, probably relieved to get a break from the interview. Sigurdís and Garðar stood up, and together they went from room to room. It was obvious that little housework had been done over the last few days. There was mess in every room. In the kitchen, Sigurdís saw a broken wine glass lying on the floor, beneath a red splash on the wall. She pointed it out to Garðar, who said that it was red wine, probably. Moving into the bathroom, they saw that the shower curtain had been torn down and its rail lay on the floor, the plastic heaped on top of it.

Garðar frowned questioningly at Sigurdís, then walked back into the living room. 'Did Óttar actually visit you on Wednesday?' he asked Erla. 'Did he come here, and was there ... a disagreement between the two of you?'

His tone was sharper than it had been so far, and Erla looked shocked at Garðar's questions.

'No. No, he didn't. We only spoke on the phone.' The phone company should be able to confirm, thought Sigurdís and made a mental note to check.

'So what happened here?' Garðar pressed. 'Why's the shower curtain on the floor, and why does it look like someone threw a wine glass at the wall in the kitchen?'

Erla stood up and went to the window, looking away from them as she said, 'I was looking at a picture of us together and I was so furious at what has happened, I smashed the glass against the wall. I was going to see if a shower would calm me down, but ended up wanting to just curl up in the bottom of the bath. I caught the curtain as I collapsed.' She spun round to face them now. 'Look, I haven't been able to sit, stand or lie down since this nightmare began. It's all so unreal.'

Garðar put his hands out in a placating gesture. 'We understand, we really do,' he said, his voice back to his previous calm tone. 'Is there a priest you'd like us to contact for you? Someone else we could call?'

'No. My friends are all coming over later on. They're worried about me because I haven't been answering the phone. So they sent a text telling me that they're all coming together this afternoon, and I can't escape them.' She shrugged helplessly.

Sigurdís sat back down on the sofa. She had a question about the days leading up to the death, and she thought it was the right time to ask it. 'Has there been anything about Óttar's behaviour that has attracted your attention recently? Anything he might have been worried about?' She noticed a little nod from Garðar as he observed Erla carefully.

'No. But, you know he had been noticeably affectionate and cheerful. I was convinced there was a proposal on the way, or at least a suggestion that we move in together. We were so well suited – or so I thought. He was the love of my life. I know I've told you that already, but it's true.' She turned to gaze out of the window as if looking into a world of her own. 'I felt that life was going so well for us ... But somehow it never seems to pan out as you imagine.'

Erla slumped down into a chair before continuing.

'One thing we had in common was that Óttar and I both grew up without a father. My father had two girlfriends when he got my mother pregnant. The other girlfriend got pregnant at around the same time, and that was when she found out that she wasn't the only woman in my father's life. So she gave him an ultimatum, and in the end, he chose her over my mother, and they're still married today. Mum cut off all communication with him and moved in with her brother in Höfn in Hornafjörður, which was where I was born and grew up. Mum's brother and his wife had been living there for a few years already, and they had a daughter who was a year older than me. They helped Mum enormously. We had a lovely flat in the basement of their house that my uncle fitted out for us. We were all very close – my cousin and I were brought up like sisters.'

Erla stopped a moment, put a hand to her face and blinked several times. 'But then my uncle and aunt split up. She moved to Reykjavík, taking my cousin with her. I missed her terribly because we had always been so close. And then...' Erla stopped, coughed. Her face twitched. 'And then she died. She fell in with a bad crowd of youngsters here in the city. And things turned from bad to worse until ... until she was found dead ... And now it's all happening again...' And with that she again dissolved into tears.

Sigurdís could feel the old stone in her gut. This poor woman, who was so beautiful, but living with so much misfortune. She looked over at Garðar and saw that he was getting restless. He had clearly decided it was time to go. He moved over to Erla and placed a hand lightly on her shoulder, telling her she would be welcome to get in touch if she had any questions, or if anything that might be useful to the investigation were to come to mind.

9

Óttar's apartment was in the Shadow District, a beautiful place on the eighth floor with magnificent views over the mountains and ocean to the north and over Reykjavík's city centre to the west.

Sigurdís, along with Garðar and Unnar, had joined the forensics team, who were trying to find anything that could be useful to their investigation. The apartment was covered in a wide selection of fingerprints as the surprise birthday party had taken place here and it had been crowded with people. Anything they found would therefore be of little use. But Erla had given them a guest list so they could speak to all those who had been present. Apparently they were the people Óttar generally spent time with.

It seemed that everything had been cleared away after the guests had left. In the kitchen, which opened onto the dining area and living room, they found the fridge piled high with bizarre canapés, while a stack of clean plates and a box of glasses stood on the counter.

The flat was otherwise very neat – maybe typical of a single man about to embark on marriage to his long-term girlfriend. There were no photographs of people, other than one of Óttar with Erla. Instead, the walls were hung with tasteful works – mostly by familiar artists. The furniture was the best that money could buy. Everything was white, black, or in smoky-coloured oak. The whole place had the feel of being a show apartment from a brochure – impersonal and very elegant.

The main bedroom was grand and, like the living areas, it had few things indicating someone lived there full time. Sigurdís stepped into the large walk-in wardrobe.

'He must have been a total clothes freak,' she said. 'Everything's colour-coordinated.' A row of shirts still in the dry-cleaner's plastic wrappers hung on one rail. Ties were neatly rolled up in a drawer and even the man's underwear was folded and looked to have been ironed.

'Do you think this guy ever used a washing machine?'

Garðar glanced across at her. 'What makes you say that?'

'Well, I can't imagine he had time to iron and fold all this so neatly. I used a laundry service a couple of times before I bought a washing machine, and all this has the same smell and finish.'

'That's hardly what killed him. I'll take a look at his office. There might be something there among the papers that'll give us some leads,' Garðar said, backing out of the room.

Sigurdís felt her cheeks flush at his comment, but said nothing. Most likely she had been watching too many episodes of *Criminal Minds*, in which the focus was on using every tiny detail to create a clear picture of the victim, and thus help profile the perpetrator. Garðar clearly wasn't going down that route, and he was the one with experience of investigating murder cases. He was probably thinking that most murders take place within close relationships, or were down to conflicts rooted in booze or drugs. Occasionally business dealings might be behind the crime. But there had been no alcohol found in Óttar's bloodstream, and the location indicated that Óttar hadn't met the perpetrator at the beach by chance. In addition, his injuries indicated that it had been a violent encounter, most likely driven by anger.

'Sigurdís,' said Garðar, interrupting her thoughts. 'I reckon Unnar and I can finish up here. How about you take off home and get some rest? We have long days ahead of us on this one. We still need to finish going through the budgets to see what can be shaved off to keep us on the right side of zero this year. This investigation certainly won't help in that regard. I'll need your help on that in the morning.'

She had the impression that Garðar didn't think she would be much use in this investigation. It was clear he had only brought her along to soften the difficult conversations they'd had to have with Thrúður and Erla – make having the police in their houses easier. Then he'd allowed her to tag along here because he didn't know what else to do with her.

Sigurdís said nothing in reply to him, but decided to look around the flat one more time before she got away from the fog of testosterone.

The bathroom was as sterile as everything else. She opened the cabinets and saw carefully arranged hygiene products from Boss and other expensive brands. The man had obviously been concerned about his looks –never before had she seen such an array of ointments and creams aimed at men determined to maintain their youthful complexion. She tried to conjure up an image of the respectable civil servant, lying on the sofa with slices of cucumber over his eyes while a face pack worked its magic. There was no bathtub, but instead there was the largest shower she had ever seen. It was tiled in dark granite, with a long drain that ran right across the floor. The shower itself was something she had never seen – a single overhead shower head, and rows of horizontal nozzles arranged on three walls of the cubicle. That had to be some kind of massage thing, she decided. Sigurdís had never envied anyone their shower – until now.

'This shower's a proper Bentley. This guy knew how to do things in style,' she said as Unnar appeared in the doorway.

'Wow. Beam me up, Scotty,' he sniggered.

Sigurdís opened the cupboard under the sink and frowned. It seemed pretty shallow compared to the other cupboards she'd looked in.

'Unnar, look,' she said. 'There's hardly any depth to this cupboard. Doesn't that seem odd?'

'Not really. It's probably just because of all the pipes and stuff behind it. There must be a good few of them to power that Bentley.'

Sigurdís was on her knees, head inside the cupboard. 'The back's screwed to the wall, or whatever's behind it. Do you have a penknife? I'll try and unscrew it and see what's in there.'

Unnar was by her side, peering into the cupboard. 'Shouldn't we ask Garðar? And didn't he tell you to go on home?'

'Yeah, he did. But come on, this could be something. I want to take a quick look in there before I'm stuck behind a desk again with all the gloomy paperwork.' Unnar looked uncertain, so she persisted. 'It looks fishy to me, and I am well known for my exceptional insight...' She grinned.

Unnar smiled and added, 'Or feminine intuition? My ex used that phrase on me all the time, at least, until we split up and it stopped working.' He laughed. 'Here's the knife. Give it a try.'

Sigurdís fiddled around for a moment, trying, without success, to loosen the screws with the tool on Unnar's penknife.

'This knife's not going to do it,' she said at last. 'I need a proper screwdriver. Will you check if anyone has one?'

Unnar must have been sufficiently intrigued by the shallow cupboard, because he got to his feet and fetched a screwdriver from one of the forensic technicians who were still working their magic around the apartment, checking for fingerprints and other traces. He came back, handed her the screwdriver and she started unscrewing the back panel. It took a while, as it had been firmly fixed with eight screws – one of which was very reluctant to be loosened. But Sigurdís wasn't inclined to let herself be beaten and give Unnar the chance to make some lame joke at her expense, and finally the panel came free. She cautiously removed it.

'Hell, Sigurdís. Is that a safe?' Unnar was on his knees at her side and grinned at her. 'So feminine intuition has its uses after all?'

'Or just a basic sense of space, Unnar.' Now it was Sigurdís's turn to grin as she stared in fascination at the safe.

They called Garðar, and when he eventually appeared in the bathroom, his body language oozed irritation. They'd clearly bothered him in the middle of something, and he looked like he was opening his mouth to tell them so, when he stopped dead and stared at the safe hidden behind the cupboard.

'This was definitely concealed behind that panel?' he asked, pointing at it. Sigurdís nodded. 'So intentionally made difficult to get at – even by its owner...' he went on. 'What made you think of taking the back panel out of there in the first place?'

'Sigurdís says it's "a basic sense of space". She was suspicious of how shallow the cupboard was compared to the others,' Unnar said.

'Good work, Sigurdís,' Garðar said, a hand on her shoulder.

Sigurdís nodded again and made an effort to suppress a big grin of satisfaction.

'Now we'll need to try and open it,' Garðar continued. 'But that could be a problem. There are two locks there, both with digital codes. There must be something important inside, for him to have made such an effort to hide it and lock it up like this.' He paused for a moment in thought. 'Look Sigurdís, you'd better be on your way. I'm sorry, but someone has to go through the figures looking for cutbacks and you have a sharp eye. Go home and get some rest, so you can make a start on it with fresh eyes tomorrow. We'll finish up here.'

10

The media had been full of news about Óttar's death the whole weekend. Social media was awash with messages of sympathy for his family and friends; people recalled a good man – reliable, and a potential political leader.

On Sunday, Garðar had called Helgi, the permanent secretary, and arranged to meet him the following morning.

Helgi received Garðar in his office, which was situated in Arnarhvoll, a grand old building right in the centre of Reykjavík old town. It sat beside Arnarhóll – a small hill on which stood a statue of Ingólfur Arnarson, the first Norse settler, recognised to have reached Iceland in the year 874 with his wife, Hallveig Fróðadóttir. The building was one of the landmarks in this part of the city centre, along with the Central Bank building, the National Theatre and the prime minister's office. Garðar had never been inside Arnarhvoll, though, and was surprised to see how cramped and dated the magnificent structure was on the inside. It was a relief, though, to see that the image of ministry elites working out of spacious offices, lavished in luxury, while they pushed others to keep a tight budget was just a myth. This was no better than anything the police had to suffer at the old station on Hverfisgata. If anything, this place was even stuffier. Even the permanent secretary's office was tiny – smaller even than Garðar's own. But it was kept very neat and tidy compared to his workspace, considering the number of things that must pass across this man's desk every day.

The media had already broken the news that Óttar's death had been caused by a heavy blow to the head, and was therefore being treated as murder, so once they were sitting down, Garðar quickly brought Helgi up to date on the pathologist's findings: after the blow to the head, Óttar's side had been kicked repeatedly with great force. The broken tibia had probably occurred when he fell on the rocky shore following the blow to his head. His leg had been caught between rocks, resulting in the break. He had also received scratches to his left cheek and his cheekbone had been smashed.

'We're all in shock here,' said Helgi. 'There's a priest coming in later, and bereavement counsellor, who will speak to all the staff. Everyone liked Óttar. He'd established himself here – made something of a special position for himself in the time he had been with us.'

Helgi had been a civil servant for a long time, and he fitted his respectable but slightly dated environment perfectly. He was a tall, slim man with immaculately combed grey hair and an amiable presence; but he also bore the hallmarks of someone who had been working intensively for a long time. He was around Garðar's age, with retirement within sight. Garðar felt a rush of sympathy for him and was a bit embarrassed for having thought so badly of him over the cuts that had to be made. They weren't Helgi's decision, even though it was his job to enforce them.

'There's nobody who comes to mind who could have had a grudge against Óttar?' Garðar asked.

'He could be a tough customer, and he didn't shy away from taking on challenging work for the ministry. But at the same time, he knew that doing things the way he wanted them done took time, so he didn't apply pressure to anyone, and he was invariably courteous in his behaviour. That's where "The Panther" nickname came from. There was nothing negative about that nickname, it was just that he could be completely charming and before you knew it, the matter would be settled in the way he wanted. It goes without saying that not everyone would be overjoyed, but that's how the civil service works. Not everyone's happy with us. Our role is to ensure that tax revenue is spent responsibly, that budgets aren't exceeded and that parliament's decisions are acted upon. You'll be familiar with that in the police.'

Garðar had prepared himself well for this meeting, aware that he would have to ask difficult questions of someone who had financial power over his department.

'Weren't state properties his responsibility?' he said. 'Acquisitions and sales? Could any business of that kind have left a bad taste somewhere?'

Helgi glanced out of the window for a moment before replying.

'I fail to see how his work here could have someone wanting him dead. He was appointed six or seven years ago. He was an interesting character. Before he came to us, he had been prominent in the public debate around the financial crisis. He worked as an independent consultant and quickly became one of the media's most popular pundits on the subject. He was critical of the government, but he was admired because his stance crossed party lines. He spent a lot of time warning of the possibility of corruption, mostly connected to the resale of the assets that were coming into state hands as the failed banks were being wound up. He spoke passionately about it – he said there needed to be full transparency around the sales of these assets.'

Garðar remembered this well. The widespread admiration for Óttar's rhetoric had led to a web page being set up, urging him to stand for parliament. Several thousand people had signed the petition attached to the site.

Helgi cleared his throat and continued. 'He was extremely

popular in the community too, although my personal view was that his rhetoric could be on the populist side at times. So it was a surprise to see he'd applied when the position of a specialist adviser with the ministry was advertised. But he presented an excellent CV, so we asked him in for an interview. He told us that he felt he could be of more use in the civil service than in politics. He said he was unhappy with all the personal attention he was getting and wanted to withdraw from the public debate. So when he saw this position advertised, he jumped at the opportunity.'

Garðar listened with interest. It was true – Óttar had vanished from the media as suddenly as he had appeared on all the TV debates and news programmes.

'The whole process and the list of applicants was public,' Helgi continued, 'so word got out immediately that Óttar was one of the applicants. Public opinion was that the ministry would be lucky to have him. People even went so far as flooding us with emails, encouraging us to employ him. Ultimately the feeling here was that appointing him would improve public trust in our work, at a time when we were getting to grips with complex issues. And ultimately, his application carried some real weight, so it was decided that he should be offered the post.' Helgi raised his hands for a moment, as if to say the decision had been simple. 'Once in post, he was involved in setting up working practices. His colleagues have been happy to work by them ever since.

'It wasn't all plain sailing though. In his first few months here, Ottar was very frustrated by how long it took for parliament to process issues.'

Garðar could relate to that feeling – as could probably most people outside government.

'He was impatient with the heated debates in parliament and the endless filibustering, but he quickly learned that good things come to those who wait, and he understood the importance of these matters being subject to democratic scrutiny.' Helgi fell silent then, looking again out of the window at his side.

Garðar found it difficult to read anything into Helgi's expression as he continued to gaze at the statue of Ingólfur Arnarsson outside his office.

'We need to turn every stone, Helgi,' Garðar said. 'I need a complete list of all the issues Óttar is or has been involved in, and I need your permission to speak to your staff.'

Helgi glanced at Garðar with a stern look on his face. 'I expect we can compile such a list. But it would be preferable if you could leave questioning my staff until tomorrow, after the priest and the bereavement counsellor have met with them. I'll let everyone know that you'll be here in the coming days to interview them about Óttar.'

As Garðar got into his car he was already starting to regret agreeing to Helgi's request that he should wait until the next day to interview Óttar's ministry colleagues. But what was done was done, so he decided to let it go.

On the way to the station, it occurred to him that approaching the political figures Óttar had worked with over the past few years might help the investigation. This meant talking to a large group of people, as there had been frequent changes in government in recent years. Garðar reckoned that Óttar must have worked with ministers from four different parties. He felt a tingle of anticipation when he thought about interviewing these people. He imagined many of them would have opinions very different from those held by Óttar, a man who trod his own path and who had been both an aggressive pundit and a forthright critic of Iceland's politicians prior to joining the ministry. His appointment must have really grated with some of them.

✻

Back at the station, Garðar called his team for a meeting.

'I've spoken to the permanent secretary and tomorrow it's best if Unnar, Viktor and I go to the ministry to talk to the staff. That'll take all day, as there are close to a hundred people there. We'll prioritise them, beginning with Óttar's closest coworkers in his department. From there we'll go to the heads of other departments, and so on. Sigurdís, I want you here to continue with the work on the cuts, but I'd also like you to keep on top of the technical people who are trying to open Óttar's safe. Don't hesitate to push them hard – call them regularly and ask for updates.'

'Brilliant,' Sigurdís snapped back. 'I get to be the passive-aggressive bitch. That's exciting, thanks,' she finished with mock delight. She wanted to be at the heart of this investigation. She couldn't help her sarcasm. She didn't appreciate being put in the corner, particularly when she had been the one to find the safe.

Garðar let her comment pass, and went on to say that while the crime-scene technicians continued combing through every possible item they had found, he, Unnar and Viktor would continue to research the contents of Óttar's work laptop and his home computer. The two devices did not appear to be connected and there were different sets of documents on each, in addition to which he appeared to have been using more than one email address.

Sigurdís left the meeting room and headed for the bathroom. She needed to splash a bunch of water on her face to stop herself from screaming in frustration. When she was done, she called Dóra, asking her to meet for sushi somewhere so she could let off steam about the boys' club.

11

The sushi joint on Tryggvagata in downtown Reykjavík was packed. Dóra hadn't turned up yet, so Sigurdís asked to be put on the waiting list for a table. A cheerful young waiter told her there was about a fifteen-minute wait, and as Dóra was invariably a quarter of an hour late, that fit perfectly.

Muted music carried through the chatter in the place as Sigurdís waited at the bar, glancing around. She noticed a young couple who looked as if they had been plucked from a cheesy chick-flick. Their fingers were entwined over the table as each gazed lovingly into the other's eyes. They had hardly touched their food.

Although her parents' relationship had been toxic, Sigurdís knew that they had been in a minority – that dark minority of violent marriages. Still, she had never yet found the confidence to allow herself a relationship of her own. She'd always retreated whenever someone she was seeing wanted to take things further than just a few casual hook-ups. The best result was when they simply didn't call again. That way there was nothing to worry about. She didn't do formal dates, and flatly refused to go on the blind dates that her girlfriends were so keen to set up for her. She would meet guys at bars, and if they weren't too drunk or their pick-up lines weren't too corny, she might agree to meet them later. Her conditions were clear, though: any contact had to be informal, among friends and in a relaxed setting. But the more often she saw a guy, the brighter the flaming stone in her belly burned, and to rid herself of the feeling, she would cut him off completely. Besides, none of the guys she'd met this way had come across as being in any way exceptional. And she had never been in love.

Maybe I'm just emotionally blocked, she thought to herself. All the same, at times she did let herself dream of having a beautiful relationship and a close family.

Her phone rang, pulling her from her thoughts. It was her brother Einar.

'Hi, my love, how are you?' she asked cheerfully.

'I'm great,' Einar replied. 'Haven't seen you for ages. Why don't you come for dinner with me, Halla and Gunnar sometime this week? We can have a chat.'

'Yes, of course I will. It'll be good to see you all.'

'There's another thing: I have a history exam coming up and it would be brilliant if you could go through some notes with me. Can't keep my mind on it, somehow. Would you mind helping?'

'Not at all.' Sigurdís smiled to herself. 'How's Halla? All fine with her?'

'Yeah. Spoiling me as usual. She just bought me a new computer. Oh, and I forgot to tell you: I found some weekend work at a restaurant downtown. I am really enjoying it. It's always full of tourists, so I can practise my English and earn a bit of cash so I don't have to keep asking Halla for money – to go to the cinema or buy clothes and whatever.'

'So pleased to hear it, sweety. Just take good care of yourself and don't overdo it.'

'Sigurdís! Don't worry so much – I'm twenty-one. I've only got three more terms at college and I'll be finished. A grown-up at last!' he said with a laugh. 'I think I'm doing well now. It feels like I'm finally getting the hang of the studies. But I need to find my way out of the cotton wool that you and Halla keep me wrapped up in.'

Hearing her brother so positive and happy gave Sigurdís a warm glow inside, and she couldn't stop herself grinning widely. 'I know. Sorry. But you're my little miracle and you're so incredibly important to me ... How about we go and see a movie at the weekend? We've got so much to talk about. There's a big case going on right now that you might have heard about – a murder case. I'm trying to get involved in the investigation but they seem to think I'm a delicate little thing and keep giving me clerical work – except when they need a woman with them for interviews and dealing with relatives.'

'So, are we both trying to escape the cotton wool that the people around us swaddle us in? See where I'm coming from now?' Einar said, and they both laughed.

'Looking forward to seeing you soon,' said Sigurdís, 'and give Halla a kiss from me.'

Einar had made an astonishing recovery from his injuries, which the doctors had attributed to his young age. All the same, he had missed a great deal of his early education, so high school hadn't been easy for him. He had taken a two-year break, until Sigurdís and Halla had between them persuaded him to resume his studies. But he seemed to have benefitted from that time away.

On a social level, he kept things low-key, spending much more time in front of a computer than on night life. He had started CrossFit training, which seemed to suit him, and he was spending time with lads his own age he had got to know through training. Sigurdís had often wondered whether to suggest he move in with her, but Halla had been so good to him – as she had been to her – and there was no good reason to disrupt an arrangement that worked so well. Halla provided him with a stable home life, and her husband Gunnar was a fine role model for Einar.

Sigurdís had been waiting for twenty minutes when Dóra bustled through the doors.

'Hi. Sorry I'm late. No free tables?'

'I'm used to your impeccable timing, and we'll get a table in a few minutes,' Sigurdís replied. 'I had a chat with Einar while I was waiting, so no problem. Haven't spoken to him often enough recently.'

'How is he?'

Sigurdís filled Dóra in on how Einar was doing at school, and about his weekend restaurant work.

'He's such a sweetheart. He sees nothing but the good in everyone, in spite of everything,' Dóra said with affection in her voice, just as the waiter appeared to let them know that their table was ready.

'Now, I need a glass of red wine. It's been a lousy day. Could I order a glass right away?' she asked the waiter, adding that Sigurdís would no doubt want a Diet Coke. 'Isn't that right, darling?'

Sigurdís nodded, even though she would have preferred water. She knew Dóra would be happier if there was something with some colour in Sigurdís's glass, keeping her own company. Dóra was unusually excited and Sigurdís sensed that she had news she couldn't wait to pass on.

'Mum and Dad have decided to sell their holiday home! You must have noticed when we were detoxing there last year how little the place has been used in the last few years and how overgrown the land around it has become. Well, they've decided to split the proceeds between me and my brother Ari so that we each have enough for a down payment on a flat and can get out of that extortionate rental market. Isn't that brilliant? I've started house-hunting already. I just went to see a place. It's in the western part of the city, and it was a proper hole, considering the price, so now I'm looking in Norðurmýri and even around Háaleiti. There are decent places there for slightly less, and I can always cycle into town. Since I'm working in the Kringlan mall, these neighbourhoods are withing walking distance, so that could be perfect. Could even ditch the car and close off that drain on my budget.'

'That's great news. They really look after you,' Sigurdís said, sincerely pleased for her friend.

'I reckon it's just to make sure that we don't try to escape the crazy rental market by moving back home. Ari's pretty skint. But I was thinking of using part of it to make an old dream come true and take a trip to New York in the autumn. You must come too. You're so sensible with money, I know you can afford it. Can you imagine chilling in the Big Apple, eating gorgeous food and enjoying that crazy city. What do you say?'

Sigurdís hesitated. 'I'm not sure how it would fit in with work,' she said. 'Although I'm sure my colleagues would be delighted if I were to take some time off.'

Dóra knew her well and clearly had no intention of taking no for an answer. 'Aren't you always telling me that they don't know what to do with you? Has that changed – are you investigating that murder, the man who was found on the beach?'

'Yes. Well, at any rate it was my job to inform his family that the body had been found, and I was part of the team examining his home. In fact, I had a bit of a coup there – I found a safe, hidden in a place nobody else had thought to look. But they still sent me home in the end, and tomorrow I'm back to clerical duties while they interview his colleagues and start looking at all his paperwork and work through his computers and email accounts. He'd received threats, apparently. They haven't managed to open the safe yet, so we don't know yet how important finding that might be. But the whole situation is driving me crazy. Garðar's clearly still eaten up with guilt over me and Einar. It was all right when I was working shifts, but after I lost it with that bully downtown, they're not putting me back on the beat again for the foreseeable. So all that's left is shuffling paper.'

'You need to make yourself indispensable. Start digging on your own account. I don't know many people who are as sensitive as you are to other people's feelings. Couldn't you tell Garðar that you want to shadow him through the investigation –so you can learn from the master? Play a little on his ego maybe?'

'That's actually not such a bad idea,' Sigurdís replied, grateful for sound advice from her oldest friend. 'I'll see if I can find an opportunity. But first I need to complete this cutbacks report for him – and I need to do it properly. It's definitely not a job that's going to finish itself, and I don't want him to have any reason to keep me busy on it any longer than I need to be.'

A colourful, enticing sushi platter appeared on the table between them. Sigurdís started the meal by unintentionally crossing her chopsticks so that her first piece of sushi went flying and landed on the floor. Once they had stopped laughing at what Dóra referred to as a 'movie incident', and had shared some gossip about her work colleagues, Sigurdís asked after Dóra's family.

'They're fine. Mum and Dad are like teenagers. Endless cocktail hours and dinner parties. Ari and I are hardly ever invited, but last weekend Mum finally invited us and I don't think I've ever laughed so much over dinner.'

'Tell me about it,' Sigurdís said, relieved to have shifted the conversation away from her work troubles, and from this New York trip. She suffered from a terrible fear of flying, which could be triggered simply by the mention of such a long flight. She knew that she would have to use all her cunning tactics on Dóra to avoid the trip.

'Well, there was a conversation I heard between Mum and one of her friends – she has a son who's a bit younger than me and who was a whole load of trouble into his early twenties. He was locked away for assault, drug offences and burglary. He even broke an old lady's arm and stole her handbag, and I don't know what else. Completely nuts. Anyway, he's been clean for three years now, and this friend of Mum's is over the moon with him, and goes on as if he's never put a foot wrong. Which is fine, I suppose, as he's doing well and he's really a great guy. Then I heard her complaining to Mum that the girl he's now living with and has a baby with maybe isn't the type she would have picked for him, because she hasn't really found her niche in life and isn't very well educated. What a joke! Her lad broke an old woman's arm, but this lovely girl isn't good enough because she didn't finish high school. I couldn't believe it!'

Sigurdís burst out laughing.

'She's such a snob,' Dóra went on. 'And now it's as if all that stuff just never happened and the boy never did time. At least he has his high-school certificate – which, by the way, he was able to study for in prison.'

Dóra laughed and Sigurdís had to join in. Dóra always had something amusing to recount, and spending time with her was a sure-fire way of ensuring that all the day's unpleasantness evaporated like dew in the sunshine.

'Listen, darling,' Dóra said, as they were getting up to leave. 'Think it over about New York. I really want to go with you, but it could also be fun to invite some of the others and make it a proper girls' trip.'

'I like the idea of checking with the others,' Sigurdís said with relief. This would make it easier to get out of going, without upsetting Dóra and ensuring she wouldn't be travelling alone. 'Put a message on the Facebook group tonight and see who's up for it.'

'OK. Give me hug, tough guy, and good luck dealing with Garðar. I have faith in you. You're so sensitive and so intuitive that I reckon they need you for this investigation.'

'Thanks, Dóra. It's good to know someone believes in me.

Let's chat with the girls on Facebook and talk after. Give your mother a big hug from me.'

'Will do. She'd love to see you. We'll get ourselves into one of their parties sooner or later. We'll definitely find something to talk about there,' Dóra said with a laugh, and strode out into the evening sunshine.

12

Garðar, Unnar and Viktor had spoken to around twenty of Óttar's coworkers, and were little the wiser for their efforts. When they compared notes, they agreed that nobody seemed to have known Óttar well on a personal level. However, it seemed that the younger staff looked up to him, describing him as a genius negotiator who always got what he wanted. It was clear they had a great deal of respect for him, and that he'd fitted in well at the ministry and spoke well of everyone. Nobody they interviewed could recall any incident that had left anyone so bruised that they would have wanted him dead. Aldís, the only female coworker they had interviewed so far, even described him as a brilliant networker, making an appearance at every gathering and conference as if he were a presidential candidate. He left nobody out, shook every hand and didn't spare the compliments.

Garðar had interviewed his closest colleague, Arnar, who had been Óttar's right hand man for two years. In his early thirties, he seemed devastated by the news of his boss's death.

'We're all in shock here,' he said. 'I can't get anything done. I just walk around the place like a ghost.'

Garðar gave him some time to collect himself before asking about the projects Óttar and he had been involved in.

'Right now we're mostly working on selling properties that are in poor condition. The current administration is pushing their policy on a paperless and more digitalised work environment, with fewer square metres of office space, which means we need more flexible workspaces. These old institutional buildings with their thick walls often just don't meet these modern requirements. So we've been assessing which properties can be modified and which ones can't, and therefore need to be sold. Óttar seemed to be fully on board with this policy. He often said we need to drag ourselves into the twenty-first century and not get left behind, mouldering. He wasn't entirely on the same page as the minister, though, on how to best implement the policy. Óttar wanted to sell off as much as possible and lease new offices from private investors. He said that would make government operations more flexible. But the government still wants to own the buildings it uses. There are examples where the state has got itself locked into long-term commitments to lease expensive buildings from the private sector, which explains its position. So, yes, Óttar and the Budgetary Committee didn't agree – on this at least.'

Arnar paused for a moment, covering his face with both hands before looking back up at Garðar sighing. 'Ach, sorry. I'm rambling on about things of no importance. I just want to give you an idea of what goes on here. It probably makes no difference to your investigation.' Arnar sounded despondent. 'I can't imagine that anyone could have been that angry with his position on governmental offices that...'

He looked to be about to break into tears, so Garðar decided that enough was enough. He asked Arnar if he could get back to him when the police had been through the files relating to Óttar in greater detail.

'Sure. What's your number? I can give you a call if I remember anything. My head's all over the place right now.'

Garðar handed him a card, and then directed the focus of the interview onto Óttar's personal life.

Arnar fell back in his chair before answering and ran his fingers through his hair.

'He seems to have been devoted to his fiancée, Erla. He was really sweet to her – he regularly sent flowers to her at work. She's a lawyer in a legal practice. She's nice – and quite like him in a way. She's good-looking, always well dressed and elegant – like the types you see in magazines: always impeccable. I haven't met her often, just the few times she attended some events with him. He didn't talk much about the other people in his life, though. I suppose he liked to keep his personal life to himself.'

'How about other women, before Erla came along?'

'I don't recall any. I'd only been working here a few months when they got to know each other.'

Garðar realised he wasn't going to get much more out of Arnar, so he wound up his questioning, and with all the relevant interviews now complete, Garðar decided to return to the station to go through the paperwork they had collected from the ministry.

As he drove away from the building, he went over the papers in his mind. There were a few intriguing items there. Among the dry-as-dust memos and reports was a list of the property sales Óttar had been involved in. Some of these had been the subject of media attention, as often as not generating uproar, as the buildings were of cultural significance. Garðar also noticed that Óttar had written numerous memos and emails suggesting the sale of assets other than buildings. His opinion was that it was not acceptable for the state to own companies that were in direct competition with the private sector.

To Garðar this sounded sensible enough, but he wondered how qualified he was, as a policeman, to develop an informed opinion on all these sales. He decided that he'd need to seek advice from someone in the financial-crime division on what the team had found in these papers. They might be able to put a finger on something that could point them in a useful direction.

✳

'Listen up, please, everyone,' Garðar said as the team hurriedly came together for a case meeting. 'I'm bringing in some support from the financial-crime division to work on Óttar's papers. They understand the business lingo better than we do and might notice something we've overlooked. Nothing's out of the question now. Viktor and Unnar, you're with me on going through his emails in detail. I reckon it's worth checking to see if he trod on anyone's toes when he was giving his opinions on the state of the country in the aftermath of the financial crisis and before he dug himself into ministry paperwork. If I recall correctly, he wasn't shy about expressing himself about various issues, and about various people in business and politics. That could have affected someone. Sigurdís, could you set up an additional work area for the financial crimes guys, so it's ready when they get here?'

Sigurdís nodded, although the request irritated her. Her thoughts went back to Dóra encouraging her to play her cards right.

'Could I have a quick word with you in private?' she asked Garðar as the meeting broke up.

He nodded and they went over to his office.

'Since Thorgeir signed me off,' Sigurdís began as soon as the door was closed, 'I've been wondering about my position within the force and where to go from here. I've always liked being on the beat, but since being with your team, I'm more and more excited about taking part in investigations like this one.'

She paused. Garðar seemed to be lost in his own thoughts, and she wondered if she'd chosen a bad moment for this conversation. Her inner critic shook its head at her awful timing, but she ignored it, knowing she had to continue what she'd started.

'I'm still badgering the boys over the safe. They got it off the wall, found the manufacturer and have contacted them in Germany to seek assistance. So how about I finish the cutbacks report, which is coming along well now, and then join you on this case? I really want to learn, and not least from you. I won't get under your feet and I'll do whatever's needed.'

Garðar stared at her hard, apparently thinking it over.

'All right, Sigurdís,' he said at last. 'That sounds fine. Finish the cutbacks job and then you can come in to support the team.'

Sigurdís smiled. 'Thanks. You won't regret this, I promise.'

Although she had doubted herself a few minutes earlier, she now sensed some kind of relief from Garðar. Perhaps he'd realised her suggestion would allow him to keep her under his wing. She knew that after the incident downtown he had fought back against the instincts of the more senior ranks, which were to get rid of her, and that he'd been driven mostly by the guilt he felt over her father. She was reluctant to play on this even further, but decided she could push it just a little more, at least until she was being taken more seriously. She was aiming for a police career now, after all.

She walked out of his office determined to give this investigation everything she had, and push herself upward in the process.

13

'Garðar, they've opened the safe!' Sigurdís called out as she burst in on the morning meeting taking place in the incident room.

'Great news,' Garðar replied. 'Did they say anything about the contents?'

'Not yet,' Sigurdís replied. 'I gave the technical team strict instructions not to touch anything inside the safe. I told them everything would have to be checked for fingerprints or other forensic evidence to establish who might have handled the contents, in case that turns out to be important.'

'Excellent. Call forensics and ask someone to meet you at the apartment to fetch what's inside the safe. We'll go through it here so we won't be disturbing the apartment any more than we already have. And that way we'll also save ourselves some time going back and forth.'

Sigurdís was happy to have received this task, and immediately went to call forensics. Then she grabbed her jacket and rushed out to her car.

'Well, we did it in the end,' said the elated young technician. Sigurdís knew he'd been working with the manufacturer without a break to open the safe. 'I didn't touch anything once we had cracked the locks, just like you said. Didn't dare leave a fingerprint behind in case I'd be a suspect,' he grinned.

'Fantastic job. Many thanks. Go home and get some rest. You've earned it,' she said.

She snapped on some gloves and cautiously opened the door of the safe. The contents took her by surprise, even though she hadn't formed any specific ideas about what might be in there. There were stacks of banknotes – bundles of five-thousand-króna and hundred-dollar notes. Sigurdís had never seen so much money in one place. The safe also contained memory sticks, envelopes and documents.

When the forensics team arrived a few minutes later, she couldn't contain her curiosity and stood close by, holding her breath as they packed everything into a big plastic container.

Sigurdís held back her excitement as she carried the container out to her car. She knew that Garðar and the team were keen to know what the safe contained, but she couldn't resist having her own look at the contents ahead of the others, so at the first opportunity on the way back to the station, she pulled over at a drive-through place. She was still wearing the gloves she'd put on at the apartment, so was able to carefully examine each item in the container.

Apart from the money – she had no idea what it might add up to – she found a stack of transfer receipts from the Chase Bank in the USA. The first was from August 2004, and the last was dated September 2008. They were for amounts from a thousand dollars up to three thousand, paid into an account at Chase over those four years. There were also two memory sticks and a bundle of documents that looked to be contracts.

Her attention was also drawn to a creased slip of paper. It appeared to have been crumpled up and then flattened out again. There was a phone number on it, beginning with +1, so it had to be an American number.

'What's so important about these transfers that they need to be so carefully hidden. And who hides a phone number in a locked, hidden safe?' she muttered to herself.

She decided to note down the key information on the transfer receipts, and also the phone number, just in case she didn't get to be involved in investigating the contents of the box.

Her phone rang; Halla's name was on the screen.

'Hi, sweetheart,' she said. 'You'll be working, so I'll get straight to the point. Could you get in touch with Einar? Ideally come and see him? He's been like he's seen a ghost these past couple of days, like he's had a shock of some kind. Have you spoken to him recently?'

'Not since Tuesday evening. He suggested I come over for dinner sometime soon. But I've been so busy, I forgot to call you to arrange it. He was fine when I spoke to him – happy with school and this new job he's found.'

'Exactly. He's always so positive and cheerful that I'm wondering whether something's happened. I'm worried about him. Have you heard anything from your mother?'

'No. Nothing more than our usual courtesy calls on her birthday and at Christmas. Apart from that, she doesn't call me any more than I call her. But you know all about that. Why do you ask?'

'Ach ... Just wondering if she had been calling the two of you and if that might have upset him.' Halla paused for a moment, as if thinking what to say. 'Look, I don't always tell you this, but I do call her regularly. And visit her too. She's my sister, after all, and life hasn't been kind to her. So I feel I need to check up on her and make sure she's coping with everything. But there's nothing to report really. She's been fine recently. She talks about some TV serial she spends half of every day watching. So she's doing something, even if she rarely goes out. And she seems to be taking her medication. I just worried that she might have spoken to Einar and that would explain his mood. Anyway,'

Halla seemed to dismiss her own concerns, 'you're busy, and I have to run myself. Please try and get hold of Einar. I'm not getting through to him.'

Sigurdís knew that Halla had long been concerned that her sister bore a grudge against her for applying for, and getting custody of, her and Einar. This was despite their mother's doctor making it clear to them that she felt that after what had happened, she didn't deserve to have children and accepted that it was best for them to be with Halla. At the time it was considered that she was so ill with depression and some kind of PTSD that she was in no state to look after them anyway. Sigurdís remembered feeling relieved that her mother hadn't put up a fight; there was no doubt in her mind that Einar would have gone to her if she had asked him to. He was so good-natured, he wouldn't have wanted to cause his mother even more distress by leaving her. He also recalled little of what had happened to him, so didn't blame her for any of it, as Sigurdís did.

But she had to give her mother credit for having their best interests at heart when she agreed they should live with Halla. *She did the right thing for us in the end*, Sigurdís thought.

She heard her phone ping and saw a text message from Viktor:

What is taking you so long?

She hurriedly put everything away, started the engine and set off, with the box at her side, which she hoped would provide some clue as to what had happened to Óttar.

03.04.1995

Mum is leaving for her trip tomorrow. I can't wait. I can be with Mr Sweet the whole weekend!!

* 14 *

She had asked Einar to meet her for dinner that evening at a Thai restaurant not far from the station. He had hesitated to accept, but Sigurdís had convinced him that she needed a decent meal that could keep her going at work, since she would undoubtedly be staying on late into the night.

'My treat,' she told him, as he had finally accepted to meet her at six-thirty.

When she arrived, he was already seated at a small table by the window , drinking a glass of beer.

'Someone is indulging himself...'

Like her, Einar wasn't keen on alcohol, so she was surprised seeing him with a beer.

'Ach, yeah. Just felt like one for a change to see if it'd help me relax. I have work at the restaurant this weekend, and all that.'

Sigurdís didn't want to mention Halla's concerns that Einar hadn't been himself the last couple of days. She knew that wouldn't get him to open up. She decided to wait until he had relaxed enough for her to find out what was troubling him. There was always the possibility that Halla was reading too much into his changed mood, and that he was simply tired or something.

'Shall we go for our favourite – pad thai? I'll have the chicken, and prawns for you?' Einar asked, showing no inclination to even look at the menu.

Sigurdís agreed with a smile. Einar could be quite set in his ways, so she opted to stay with him in their safe culinary corner.

'So, how are things with you? Do you have a long weekend shift ahead of you?' she asked after they had ordered their food.

'Yes, tomorrow and Sunday. Four to midnight.'

'Wow, that's long. I hope you like the people you're working with, seeing as you'll be spending so much time with them?'

'They seem nice. Not that I've got to know them much yet. I'm still in training, but everyone is being very helpful.'

'What's the pay like? Good?'

'In my world it is. Halla thinks it's just small change, but I know I'm being paid the going rate. It's pretty much minimum wage, I think. But I'm doing something at least. Getting out of the infamous cotton wool and treading my own path.'

'Well, I think that's a great attitude. And you seem happy, and that's what it's all about. Any thoughts yet about what you want to do after college?'

'No, nothing serious yet. I like messing around with computers, so maybe computer science or something related to that.'

'That sounds great, you've always been a wizard when it comes to technology. Which reminds me, could you come round and set Netflix up for me? I'm told it's the latest thing...'

'The latest thing? You're such a dinosaur. Netflix is standard in every home and has been for a long time. Are you sure that you're ready for this huge step into the great technological evolution?' Einar asked with a sarcastic laugh.

'Now you're taking the piss. But yes I'm ready to open this whole new chapter and embrace the digitised twenty-first century.'

'We've already had nineteen years of the twenty-first century. Who are you, my grandmother?'

They shared a laugh. Sigurdís was happy to hear how upbeat Einar was, so took his jokes on the chin, even though they were at her expense. She couldn't sense any of the gloom that Halla had been worried about.

When the food arrived, they ate without saying much. The place was quiet, and the aroma of Asian spices created a pleasant enough atmosphere. Then, halfway through the meal, Einar put down his chopsticks, picked up his beer and gulped down what was left of it, while looking out the window. Normal enough, but after he had put the empty glass down on the table, she noticed his gaze remained on the window, a look on his face that she hadn't seen since they had been small and the terrifying noise from upstairs had woken him.

'Is everything all right, Einar? You seem to be having some heavy thoughts flying around in your head.'

Einar was silent. He caught her eye, opened his mouth as if about to say something, and then closed it. He stood up, spoke briefly to the waiter and then went to the bathroom. The waiter placed another beer on the table, and when Einar came back he drank it eagerly.

'Einar. Talk to me. What's bugging you?'

He took a deep breath, looked down at his hands. Clenched his fists, and rolled his thumbs rapidly in circles around each other.

'Einar, now I'm worried. Where's my happy boy gone?'

'Don't talk to me like I'm a child, Sigurdís.'

She was taken aback with his response but replied calmly: 'I'm sorry. You know we're a team and we've been through so much together. Let me share whatever's causing you so much stress.'

'I am sorry too. Of course we're a team, and that's not going to change.' He paused. Took a breath. 'Now promise me you won't overreact or do anything crazy when I tell you what's happened. I don't want you jumping up and trying to fix something for me. Some things I just need to sort out for myself. Hear me out and help me figure out what I should do next.'

Sigurdís nodded her agreement, telling herself to sit still and listen.

'I was on Facebook a couple of nights ago and noticed a message request, which means it's from someone who isn't on your friends list. The message was from someone called Daniel Christiansen. I thought it was just some spam, but then I noticed that the first couple of lines were in Icelandic.'

He stopped again. Took a deep breath.

'It was from him, Sigurdís. The old man.'

Sigurdís was stunned. She had to restrain herself from jumping up and screaming. She had promised herself and Einar that that man would never, ever, come near them again. She sat still, clamping her jaws together.

'He said he lives in Denmark and works on a farm,' Einar went on, looking at his hands. 'He hasn't married again. And he says he's ashamed of what he did. So he wants to keep a low profile. But ... but he's hoping we'll forgive him.'

Fuck Facebook, Sigurdís thought, although she knew that if the man was determined to contact Einar, he would have done so with or without Facebook.

'And what did you do?' she said, trying to control her tone. 'Did you respond?'

'No, no. I haven't yet. I was taken by surprise, of course. But I have to admit I'm very curious.'

Sigurdís stared at him, frightened to reply to this, in case the wrong words came out of her mouth.

Einar stared at her. 'Sorry I didn't bring this up earlier – on the phone or when you got here. But I just couldn't think how to tell you. It felt so wrong to talk about it out loud. To be honest, it's not something I ever expected, after everything you've told me and what little I remember.'

Sigurdís put her hands on her cheeks for a moment and took a deep breath. 'Well, I'm very glad you've not replied,' she said, managing now to keep her cool. 'Let's not answer it until we've both thought it through. There's no hurry. How about I ask around at the station – see if I can find out what he's been up to after he left Iceland? I think that would be the best thing to do.'

Einar nodded and they finished their drinks in silence, both mulling over what they'd discussed.

'I knew I'd feel better after I'd spoken to you,' Einar said as they left the restaurant. He was clearly relieved, and gave her a big hug.

'We'll deal with this together. Promise me that,' Sigurdís said, and he nodded. 'Come on. You've had a drink so I'll drive you home. I'll come and fetch you tomorrow so you can pick your car up from the restaurant.'

Sigurdís was quiet on the drive, while Einar chatted away about his CrossFit progress. The old fireball flew around in her stomach. Something was definitely brewing.

15

'Was there anything useful in the documents from the safe?' Sigurdís asked when she returned to the station after driving Einar home.

'We're just assessing that now,' Garðar said with a mild grin. 'Elín from the financial-crime unit has been looking through it all.' He gestured to the woman sitting at the workstation Sigurdís had set up earlier. 'In fact, you've arrived at the right time. She's just about to give us a digest of her findings. The floor is yours, Elín.'

Elín had a reputation for this kind of investigation. She was known for her ability to see the bigger picture, regardless of how complex it might first appear, and for being highly professional and detail-oriented, never going for a prosecution without being certain it would lead to a conviction. She was also a singularly attractive woman, with an auburn mane and large glasses. She generally seemed slightly distanced from everyday practicalities, and this was underlined by her clothes – she wore a blouse that was a little creased, a suit that was two sizes too big for her, and the lenses of her glasses were often smeared, with fingerprints at the edges. But when it came to figures and making connections, nothing escaped her. Sigurdís appreciated her attitude and thought that friends of hers who were especially particular about their appearance could learn from Elín's nonchalant style, even if only a little.

'I haven't been through the computer data,' she began, 'but

the paper documents from his safe are interesting, to say the least. To start with, it's clear that Óttar had significant assets, both here and overseas, which he owned through offshore holding companies. His name didn't appear in the Panama Papers, published a couple of years ago, so he must have taken other routes. He appears to have mainly used a legal practice in Panama called Sun & Senses Ltd. According to our sources, we can expect some revelations concerning offshore companies connected to that particular law practice at some point. It won't be long before the media get hold of the story. This is going to make the feathers fly, and there could be a backlash, especially if Óttar's holdings are included in these revelations, not least because he was responsible for the groundswell of opinion against corruption back in the day – he essentially ran a one-man fear campaign about it, if you recall. He tuned into the general distrust that the financial crash had triggered, so popular opinion was largely on his side. As was mine. So for this so-called social crusader, it would be a serious fall from grace if his financial activities were to come to light.'

Elín let all that sink in for a moment, then continued.

'The safe contained documents relating to three companies. He wasn't in this as a solo operator – there's a man called Daði Sigurðsson who is part of this as well. He's long been a significant investor here in Iceland, but we've suspected for some time that he's actually a straw man, and behind him are some very wealthy individuals. Now it seems that Óttar Karlsson might well have been one of these individuals. We found a contract stipulating that Daði gets twenty-five per cent of revenues from these operations as remuneration for ostensibly being their owner. Óttar is nowhere named as the owner of these companies, and the only mention that he is, is in this agreement between him and Daði. I need to take a closer look at this – read the contract in more detail and track down companies in Iceland that are linked to these offshore entities, as Daði has made significant investments in recent years. Up to now, we hadn't been aware of any links between Óttar and Daði. But we do know that Daði has left behind him a trail of furious former business partners and former owners of those companies who feel they were deceived when Daði acquired them. That said, we have never been able to prove these accusations, but Daði does seem to have a real talent for identifying the right companies at the right time. He started out small, but his portfolio has grown rapidly.'

Elín paused and took a sip of water before continuing.

'As we know, the state became the owner of a substantial amount of assets when the failed banks were wound up. Óttar was closely involved with shaping government policy and preparing the legislative work concerning the subsequent sales of these assets. My opinion is that this process has been largely successful and was the recipient of broad public trust, primarily because of Óttar's involvement and his background. However, the whole thing was held up in parliament by weeks of filibustering during the debates over the bill the government of the day had presented concerning the sale of the state broadcaster. As you'll recall, that particular administration collapsed after only eight months and fresh elections were called. Which delayed the legislation. What's interesting for us is that during that period, prior to the legislation being passed, four companies were sold off by the state, through a transparent tendering process. We can see from the record that Daði made offers for all four and his offer for one of them was finally accepted.'

'But how does Óttar's murder connect to his secret business dealings?' Sigurdís asked. 'Could someone have found out that Óttar was behind all this, and felt so badly betrayed that he murdered him? But in that case, why not go for Daði instead?'

'That's what I'm still figuring out, and it could well be that all we will get out of this part of the investigation is proof of tax avoidance and money laundering. Whatever else comes to light, though, it's clear that Óttar deceived a great many people – me included. I had a high opinion of this man until these documents came to light.'

Sigurdís turned this information over in her mind for a moment, but however she looked at it she just couldn't see this as a motive for murder.

'What about the other items from the safe?' she asked. 'The payments made through Chase Bank in the USA, and the phone number?'

'In the overall picture, these are small amounts. But they do raise a question about whether or not he had links in America and owed money there.'

'He was an engineering graduate from the University of Minnesota,' Sigurdís said. Then turned to the rest of the team. 'Has anyone called the number?'

Garðar replied that he had called, but there had been no reply. 'Could you follow it up, Sigurdís? Call again?'

Elín wrapped up her comments, and the team returned to their tasks.

Excited to be given the task, Sigurdís found a small meeting room, so she wouldn't be disturbed making the call to the US number. She punched the digits into the phone and a familiar knot of apprehension formed in her stomach. It took a moment for the connection to be made, and then the tones of an international phone ringing came down the line.

She waited far longer than she would normally when making a call, and was just about to hang up, when at last someone picked up the phone.

'Hello. This is Carla.'

'Hello, Carla,' said Sigurdís in reply, suddenly surprised that someone had answered. 'My name is Sigurdís Hölludóttir and I'm a police officer with CID in Iceland. I hope I'm not disturbing you?'

There was a long silence before Carla spoke again, this time in a truly stunned voice.

'Police? Iceland? What on earth could you want from me?'

'Apologies for the call, but we wanted to know if you're familiar with a man called Óttar Karlsson. We found your phone number among his effects.'

Carla again hesitated for a long time.

'Yes,' she said at last. 'I know him. We met around thirty years ago when he lived here in Minnesota.'

Sigurdís thought about this a moment. 'Can I ask what kind of relationship you had with him? Was he a friend, a boyfriend?'

'Oh, just ... We just got to know each other through a mutual acquaintance,' Carla replied, but it definitely seemed to Sigurdís like she was keen to play down her dealings with him.

'Could I ask for your surname? And do you have an account at the Chase Bank? Óttar made regular payments into one at that bank between 2004 and 2008?' As soon as these questions burst out, Sigurdís realised she was asking too much too soon. Thank God no one was listening to her diving into the conversation without properly assessing the situation.

But Carla seemed too flustered and stunned by the call to notice that Sigurdís was rushing her. She replied in a quiet voice that her family name was Abraham.

'I know nothing about all this,' she went on, 'and I can't understand why he would have my phone number.' She was still very hesitant. 'I was relieved when he left, and I wanted nothing more to do with him – not then and not now,' she finished, still in a low voice.

All Sigurdís's senses were suddenly on alert. Despite the soft tone, there was real sincerity behind Carla's words. It was clear that Óttar's name carried an emotional weight for her; but it was also clear that she was trying hard to hide it.

'Why were you relieved when he left?' Sigurdís said, immediately regretting the direct question. She found it difficult to speak to people over the phone and much preferred face-to-face conversations. It was going to be difficult to extract any information from Carla, she thought.

Carla's reply was practically a whisper, so quiet Sigurdís had to strain to hear her.

'I don't remember much about him. I didn't feel that he was a particularly pleasant person. That's all. Look, I have to go now. Sorry I can't help more.'

'Would you have any idea who owns the account he was paying into during those years?' Sigurdís rushed out, trying to keep her on the line.

She had a feeling she had a strong lead that was slipping through her fingers, all due to her own stupid impulsiveness. Why hadn't she asked Garðar to prepare her instead of diving into this phone call head first? She gulped, found a grey spot on the white wall in front of her where she set her focus, imagined it as a hole that swallowed all destructive thoughts, and felt her mind sharpen again. This was something she had done since she was a child whenever her own inner bully worked its dark magic and she felt herself getting smaller and weaker.

'No,' came the murmured answer.

Sigurdís could feel Carla shutting down. She would have to take a different track if she wanted to get anything more from her. But maybe she didn't really know anything useful. She could just be an old girlfriend and their parting hadn't been amicable. Sigurdís was certain that this wasn't the whole story, though. Why would Óttar have kept her phone number hidden in a safe all these years?

'Why are you asking me all this?' Carla asked, her whisper

surprising Sigurdís. She'd clearly wanted to end the conversation, but it seemed curiosity had got the better of her. 'Are the police looking for him; is he being investigated for something. Has he been arrested...?'

'No, no, he hasn't been arrested,' Sigurdís replied, relieved Carla was still on the line. 'I'm sorry to tell you but he was found dead recently – murdered, we believe.'

Sigurdís stopped for a moment, straining her ears for Carla's reaction. Did she just hear a quick breath?

'I'm not in a position to give you much more information at the moment,' she went on, 'except to say that while looking through his belongings as part of our investigation, we came upon your phone number and these transfers. That's why I mentioned them earlier. I was hoping you could shed some light on them.'

Sigurdís wished she was sitting in front of this woman. She could definitely hear faint breathing on the other end of the line, but she needed a facial expression, some body language to fill in the picture.

'And it would also be very helpful if you could give us a picture of Óttar's time in Minnesota...'

Sigurdís held her own breath while she waited for Carla to respond.

'I'm sorry to hear about his passing,' Carla responded, her voice suddenly cold and clear. 'Now I have to go. I'm sorry, but I can't help you. Good luck with your investigation and ... and ... just take care of yourself, OK?'

She hung up without another word. Sigurdís couldn't tell now if she had taken the news badly, or if she had been pleased to hear of Óttar's death. But one thing she did know – once Carla had heard he was dead, she had stopped whispering.

Sigurdís sat for a while in the meeting room after Carla had hung up. Her thoughts were racing and every fibre in her body was telling her that this US connection needed to be followed up. It wasn't what Carla had said, more what she hadn't that left Sigurdís feeling she needed to know more about their relationship.

*

Back in the incident room, she approached Garðar and told him she'd got through to the US telephone number.

'It's for a woman called Carla Abraham. She said she knew Óttar years ago, when he was over there.' She gave him a summary of the call, and finished up with, 'You know, I have a feeling that we ought to look at her and Óttar's time with her more closely.'

Garðar looked at her and grunted dismissively. 'Police work is based on cold, hard facts, not on feelings,' he said.

Sigurdís realised that the team had suddenly fallen silent when they heard Garðar's retort. You could have heard a pin drop.

It was Unnar who broke the uncomfortable silence, coming to her rescue. 'I'm not sure that's entirely true, Garðar. We've all long admired the way you yourself use your intuition as a starting point for an investigation – and track the cold, hard facts down from there. We need to begin somewhere, don't we?'

Sigurdís silently thanked her colleague and felt the heat vanish from her cheeks, as she sent him a grateful smile.

Garðar ran his fingers through his hair and closed his eyes as he took a deep breath. He puffed out the air as he opened his eyes. 'Yes, of course intuition has its uses, but I believe this link with America is a dead end,' he said. 'It's much more likely that the motive for the murder is connected with Óttar's involvement in these offshore companies. I think we need to work on the theory that this new leak of information Elín mentioned means someone figured out the truth about Óttar's offshore dealings. Money can drive people crazy, and that could be why he was attacked so violently. Viktor, I want you with me when we ask Daði in for questioning. Unnar and Sigurdís, tomorrow I want you two to call on Óttar's sister, Stefanía, and dig into whatever she knows about his business affairs. You can use the opportunity to ask her about his time in the US, Sigurdís. It can't do any harm.'

Sigurdís hesitated for a moment.

'Would it help to try and find out who's the holder of the account at Chase?' she asked.

'I'll ask Elín to look into that,' Garðar said gently, apparently regretting snapping at her previously. Then he picked up his jacket and left the room, with Viktor following at his heels.

When they had gone, Sigurdís turned to Unnar. 'I owe you a beer for standing up for me. '

He turned around in his chair, looked at her with his warm brown eyes and gave her a smile that could melt the most hardened criminal's heart.

'I'm taking you up on that right now. We can go to the bar at the new hotel down the road and prepare for our visit to Stefanía tomorrow morning.' He was on his feet so fast that his chair clattered to the floor behind him. Then, as he swung round to save it, he got tangled in its upturned legs and stumbled forward, almost falling to the floor as well, only saving himself by grabbing Sigurdis's shoulder.

For the second time that evening, there was a moment's pin-drop silence in the room, followed by a shout of laughter that punctured the tension. They all needed a good laugh after the strain of the last few days. Elín dabbed tears from her eyes, begging them to get out as fast as their legs would carry them so that she could have some peace and quiet to track down the owner of the Chase account.

Sigurdís and Unnar were still giggling as they left the police station. Their temperaments were very different, but she liked him a lot. He was open and straightforward, and everyone around him knew exactly where they stood with him. She'd also noticed that he never went in for subterfuge of any kind, and as his comment to Garðar had proved, he had a rare talent for encouraging others with an effortless sincerity.

Unnar was seven years her senior, of medium height, but brawny, and with a mop of wavy, light-brown hair and a few days' worth of stubble. Dóra would have called him a shabby-chic type of guy, relaxed in both his demeanour and his dress, although this look must have been artfully contrived. Today he wore jeans, a grey hoodie and a fashionable green washed-cotton jacket. Sigurdís envied his fashion sense; she'd never had any talent for clothes and always erred on the side of caution; starting with blue or black slim-fit jeans and a white T-shirt, and depending on the occasion, she either wore a hoodie, bomber jacket or black blazer. At some rare special occasions, the blazer would be a coloured one. She wore her straight blonde hair in a ponytail for every occasion – the simple option.

That morning she had opted for a grey bomber jacket, but she now wished she'd chosen a nice blazer. She felt a bit scruffy and out of place, getting a drink at a popular hotel bar – with Unnar, of all people.

'How lucky are we to live here and get to experience a bright, beautiful evening like this,' Unnar said, hauling her free of her heavy thoughts about the way she dressed.

Sigurdís looked at the streets around her. It was a bright July evening; the sun would barely set in Reykjavik that night, before it would rise again in the early hours.

He gave her a smile. 'You're an enigma, Sigurdís. You get so totally wrapped up in your own thoughts. You know, sometimes when I look at you when you're thinking, you have this expression on your face – sort of soft, but unreadable in a way. It's like you retreat into your own special place. Somewhere mystical...' He paused and looked down at the pavement. 'And I sometimes hope you will invite me with you there one day, for a visit.'

He increased his walking pace suddenly, so she fell a little behind him. Sigurdís blushed. Had he been looking at her? Her? Wanting to know what she was thinking? She couldn't find anything to say in response, not even a smartass comment. Nothing.

She was saved by the sound of low music as a guest leaving Hótel Rök held the door open for them to enter.

'This place just drips style,' she said as they went through the doors.

The lobby was unconventional – a blend of bar and reception. Instead of a reception desk manned by smiling staff welcoming the guests, there were two broad columns in the middle of the open space, each with four touchscreens where guests checked themselves in. Staff hovered in the background, bringing people drinks and snacks, or assisting guests left bewildered by the touchscreen interfaces and desperate to get to their rooms for a long-awaited rest. The decor was pleasant, and all in line with the latest interior design trends. The dominant elements were the walls lacquered in black, the exposed steel girders on the ceiling, and bronze-and-glossy velvet couches, seat covers and cushions. Large potted plants added warmth. The place was busy with both travellers and young locals, who made themselves at home on the nests of sofas. The guests appeared carefree and happy, with smiling, sun-tanned faces – a result of the unusually pleasant summer they were having this year.

Sigurdís and Unnar found a small table some distance away from the chatter and had just sat down when a girl in a stiffly pressed black jumpsuit swooped down and asked if she could bring them anything.

'I could do with a large Diet Coke,' Unnar said with a smile.

Sigurdís asked for the same, then turned to him. 'Hey, weren't you the one who was so excited at the prospect of a beer that you sent the furniture flying in your rush for the door?'

'I don't drink beer, and in general not much alcohol. My preference is Diet Coke and plenty of it. I jumped to my feet like that, because ... because it's an opportunity to spend some time with you. You've not really given your colleagues much chance to get to know you.'

Sigurdís knew he was right. There had been a few occasions when she had accompanied her colleagues on a night out somewhere, but her appearances had been fleeting at best. Rather than responding to Unnar's comment, however, she decided to change the subject – she had little inclination to shine a light on her poor social life.

'I'm just glad to get out of that awkward situation with Garðar. I know I'm not the most experienced one on the team—'

'Sigurdís,' Unnar interrupted. 'I think you're underestimating yourself. I have good friends who have worked with you and they all have huge respect for you. They say you're exceptionally talented and have a real flair for this job. One even said that you assess a crime scene better than anyone they'd worked with. Stebbi Óla told me about that time you were called out with him to a domestic incident but it was all quiet at the house when you got there – remember? He said he wanted to leave, but you had an inkling something wasn't right. He told me how you parked the patrol car out of sight and got them to quietly walk back to the house and wait. And you were right, he said. You saved that young lad from another beating from his sick mother.' Unnar paused and gave her a gentle smile. 'It's not everyone who has that kind of feel for the job, you know.'

Sigurdís was unsure of how to respond to this, and muttered

that she was pleased to hear all this – she hadn't known that the boys had told anyone about the incident.

'That's not all I've heard about you,' Unnar went on. 'Some people think you're a legend, particularly those who were downtown with you when you dealt with that bully.' He paused, still smiling. 'We were all relieved when you got to keep your job, and that the issue didn't go any further than a visit to a psychologist's office.'

'That was a hefty punishment for me,' Sigurdís said, trying to laugh it off. 'In all seriousness, though, it has been a struggle to come back after all that. I know I only kept my job because Garðar has me under his wing. So it's not been easy to look my colleagues in the eye, considering.'

Now it was Unnar's turn to laugh. 'It wasn't just Garðar who backed you up, you know. The commissioner spoke to your colleagues about you, and it was only after *those* interviews that they decided you'd get another chance.'

Sigurdís's jaw must have dropped, because Unnar made a theatrical play of catching hold of his own jaw. What he'd said had really taken her by surprise. She'd had no idea that there'd been more of a process behind the decision to keep her on the force. And the truth was, she'd dared not ask. She'd created a scenario in her own head, which, as always with her, did not put her in a positive light. And somehow she'd convinced herself that her assumptions were true. She'd clearly been very wrong.

'You're so sweet,' she said, feeling grateful and embarrassed at the same time. 'Thank you, I really needed that ... But enough about my messes. We'd better order some more Diet Coke and start getting ourselves prepared for tomorrow. That's what we came here for.'

30.04.1995

We sat together by the sea last night. We saw a ship sailing slowly into the harbour. All lit up in the dark, it looked like a circus ship, with a string of lights hanging between the masts just like the lights between the tent poles under the big top. He was sad. He's never sad. He told me it was a trawler coming in to land its catch. Trawlers are no circus ships. They take dads away from their children. I put my arms around him. We held each other tight. He promised he'd never leave me.

16

Stefanía lived alone in a small but exceptionally bright flat on the ground floor of a block in the Bakkar area of Breiðholt, one of Reykjavík's biggest suburbs, which had sprung up in the 1970s.

Her love of plants and gardening was apparent throughout the apartment.

'You obviously have green fingers. These plants are beautiful. The few I've had through the years have all given up on me and withered away,' Unnar said to her as they followed her into the living room.

'You should take a look at the balcony and the communal garden. The other residents in the block give me free rein in the gardening department. I guess they're just relieved that they don't have to do much work themselves. It's my profession, of course, landscaping advice and sales of plants. But gardening is a good place to disappear into – my peaceful little world.'

Sigurdís glanced around the neat, tasteful flat. Unlike her mother, Stefanía had a more liberal approach to colours and seemed to select items she liked rather than worrying about a strict scheme. There were a few pictures on the walls, mostly prints of drawings she recognised from the *Flora of Iceland*. There were some photographs of people, but none of her close family were visible anywhere. Sigurdís found this interesting; it had been her understanding that the three of them were close.

She decided to take the direct approach. 'I can't see any

photographs of Óttar or your mother around,' she stated as Stefanía was coming back from the kitchen with some coffee on a brightly coloured tray.

'We've never really taken many photos, and those we have are almost all at my mother's home in Ásgarður. In fact we've been going through them together these past few days.' She handed them mis-matched cups. 'Mum and I still can't comprehend what has happened. Óttar certainly had his demons, but it's beyond belief that anyone would have wanted him dead. It's hit our mother very hard. He was her golden boy. She was so proud of him.'

They sipped on their coffees for a moment, then Unnar took the lead and began to recount the information concerning Óttar's offshore holdings they had found on the items in the hidden safe in the bathroom.

Stefanía seemed genuinely surprised. 'What? I had no idea about any of this. You're telling me that he had money hidden away abroad? He certainly lived well, I suppose, and I often used to wonder how he managed it on a civil servant's salary. But then again people who live alone can allow themselves this and that even on average earnings, can't they? So I didn't think too much about it. I don't care for money that much – it's not that important to me. I'm just happy being surrounded by my plants.' Stefanía looked down at the crocheted cloth on the table. 'Of course, he was always up to something. So if I'm totally honest with you, then this shouldn't come as too much of a surprise. He wasn't like most people. He was supersmart and always cooking up schemes. He stood out in that respect.' She spooned sugar into her coffee before continuing. 'Mum always said that he had exceptional talents. She made a lot of effort as he was growing up to teach him to harness his energy and use his gifts in the right way.'

Sigurdís frowned, and asked what Stefanía meant by that.

'Ach, nothing in particular. He had an aptitude for getting people to do things for him, ever since he was small, and Mum was always worried that one day he would push things too far. But he did well for himself, so there was no need for us to worry about him.'

'Do you know Daði Sigurðsson?' Sigurdís asked flatly.

The question obviously took Stefanía off guard. 'Yes,' she said, hesitating. 'They were at primary school together for a while in Hafnarfjörður. Do you think he's somehow connected to all this? I don't think they've been in touch since they were kids – not since Daði's family moved away, from Hafnarfjörður to Akranes.'

Sigurdís explained how Daði had been involved with Óttar in business relating to these offshore holdings, and that all the indications were that Daði had agreed to be the public face of this activity, allowing Óttar to conceal his ownership of these companies.

Stefanía went pale. 'I am utterly shocked. I can't believe what you are telling me,' she said in a low voice. 'They had completely stopped communicating ... or so I thought.' She paused. 'I'm sorry, but I don't know what to say. I feel like I've stepped into some kind of alternate reality.'

Unnar laid a hand gently on her arm. 'We know this is a difficult time, but we need to find out who was responsible for his death, so we do need to ask you some more questions.'

Stefanía nodded and appeared to accept what they needed to do.

'Who were his circle of friends? Is there anyone you think we ought to be speaking to, to get a better picture of his life?'

Sigurdís could see from the look on Unnar's face that he wasn't finding it easy to apply pressure on Stefanía.

She looked up at him, now with tears in her eyes. 'I'm suddenly feeling like I hardly know anything about him.

Yesterday, when Mum and I were going through the pictures, I saw my brother. But now, after what you've told me, he feels more of a stranger.'

'Still, it would be helpful for us to know anything you can tell us about him. What about his time in America, can you talk about that?' Unnar asked.

'He went to that high-ranked university in Minnesota to do his engineering studies. He came home with a master's degree and walked straight into a well-paid job. He was always an outstanding student, there, I think, and got the highest marks.'

'And his social life in America? Do you know if he had any friends or acquaintances with whom he might have stayed in touch?'

'No, not that I know of. We weren't in touch a lot during his time there. It was expensive to call and emails weren't used by many people back then. And he didn't come home between semesters, as flying was expensive. There was one thing that happened while he was there, though...' She stared thoughtfully at one of her plants for a moment before continuing. 'At one point someone from the university called Mum, saying he hadn't shown up for his classes for a few months and that they were concerned and were looking for him. Mum went out of her mind with worry. But we couldn't find him and nor could the university. And then one day he just rang up and told her that he'd hit a wall in his studies and had decided to take a break. He said he'd got to know this interesting man from Minnesota and had travelled around the States for a while with him – just to recharge. Mum was furious he'd not told anyone where he was going. But somehow he managed to make it all seem harmless and normal. Anyway, he went back to uni, finished his studies and then he came home. So after that we didn't concern ourselves too much with what had happened over there. It's not unusual for students to experience some kind of burn-out, is it?'

'Do you know anything about this friend – or his name, at least?' Unnar asked.

'No. He never told us anything more about him, really. And I don't think he ever mentioned his name.'

Sigurdís had been waiting apprehensively to ask Stefanía about Carla. She was still a bit unsure about her timing during these interviews, realising this was a result of her lack of experience. But she judged that now seemed as good a time as any, so she decided to go for it.

'Does the name Carla Abraham mean anything to you?'

Stefanía looked at Sigurdís in astonishment. 'How ... how do you know about her?'

'So you know her, then?'

'No. Well ... I've never actually met her or spoken to her. And Óttar didn't even know that I was aware of their relationship or ... what it led to.'

Sigurdís glanced at Unnar. He was staying very still, making no effort to intervene. She realised that the best thing to do in this moment was to allow Stefanía to talk, without putting pressure on her. She let the silence stretch out, and she was rewarded. Stefanía started speaking again. She was in tears now, gritting her teeth.

'My brother was a law unto himself,' she said, drying her tears with her sleeve. 'I might as well tell you, now that he's gone. But please, can you give me an opportunity to tell Mum what I am about to tell you before you interview her again. Can you do that?' She looked at them in anticipation, a worry wrinkle forming between her eyes. 'I don't think she knows anything about ... what I'm going to tell you, and I'm not sure she'll ever forgive me for keeping it a secret.'

Sigurdís and Unnar exchanged glances again and nodded lightly.

'Yes, of course,' Sigurdís said. 'We can give you a little time to inform your mother.'

Stefanía was sitting on the edge of the couch now, and looked down for a while as if to gather her thoughts. Then she drew in a deep breath and leaned back as if she had somehow been defeated.

'Two years ago a young man knocked on my door and addressed me by my full name. And he spoke in English. So my first thought was that he had to be one of those Jehovah's Witnesses, all ready to try and sell me *War Cry* or *Watchtower*, or whatever it's called they walk these neighbourhoods with. He introduced himself as Stephen Abraham, and as I was getting ready to say "no, thank you" and close the door on him, he said he was Óttar's son. This was just out there, in the hallway.' She pointed towards her front door. 'I was thunderstruck, as you can imagine. I had no idea of his existence. I was sceptical of his claim, to say the least. But at the same time I was curious, so I invited him in. I wanted to understand what he wanted and why he was here on my doorstep, telling me this. He came in, and then he told me the story of how Óttar and his mother had got to know each other through some religious group my brother had belonged to for a while in America.' A sarcastic grin appeared on Stefanía's face, and she shot glances at them both. 'A religious group! I was speechless, because I can tell you that my brother has never been even remotely religious, and he'd never shown any indication of that changing. Stephen then told me that he didn't know much about his parents' relationship, other than Óttar had moved on before he was born. And for that reason, he wasn't sure if Óttar even knew of his existence before he'd returned to Iceland. His mother refused to discuss the matter apparently. I asked if my brother was now aware he had a son, and Stephen said yes – that he had made contact with him a few years previously. He said that Óttar had regularly sent him money, on the condition that he would not travel to Iceland and nobody was to know that they were father and son. So it was clear Óttar didn't want to know him – and the poor boy didn't dare show his face because he really needed the money Óttar sent. But he had so wanted to see where his father had come from and to meet some of his Icelandic family, he had finally made the trip. Which is why he had come to me. But he asked me not to mention this visit to Óttar. Not to say a word to him. We talked for a while, and I showed him some pictures, gave him something to eat, and then he left. I haven't seen him since. And I've kept my promise not to say anything to Óttar or Mum about him. I don't exactly know why, but I felt there was no need to make this young man's life even more complicated than it was already. He's my nephew – my little nephew – and I wanted him to know that he could trust me and come to me again.'

'So you do believe he's Óttar's son?' Unnar asked her. 'That he wasn't lying?'

'Yes. The poor kid didn't ask me for anything, and didn't seem to be after something. And ... well, I could see the resemblance.' Stefanía clenched her teeth now. 'But I also realised that my arsehole of a brother hadn't been able to do the decent thing and take responsibility for this boy – be a father to him.'

She looked down, into her lap, and Sigurdís could see that the tears were flowing again.

Unnar was strangely silent as they walked out of the building.

'Could you drive, Sigurdís?' he said at last. 'I'm not sure I can. It never occurred to me that I'd be so angry with someone who's already stone dead.'

Unnar sat in the passenger seat and glowered as he stared into the distance. He was so preoccupied that Sigurdís had to remind him to fasten his seat belt so that the multi-alarmed Volvo wouldn't ping them a warning. The last thing he needed was the constant peeping poking at his nervous system.

'It's not often that I lose faith in people,' Unnar burst out as they drove to the station. 'But this guy was a complete shit. He swindled and screwed people, gets a girl pregnant and runs away, and then bribes his son not to tell anyone about him. That's the work of a real, high-grade scumbag, if you ask me. Why do it? I'm sure Stefanía and Thrúður would have welcomed the boy with open arms, and it's not as if we live in a society where there's any prejudice against having children outside marriage. In fact, it's practically our national sport. And other thing – I don't get why he concocted this show for the media and applied to work for the government. He was wealthy enough without that job. And then why use Daði as a front? He'd have been able to do well in business under his own name...' Unnar threw his hands in the air and then let them drop.

His angry tirade made Sigurdís think.

'I agree, Unnar,' she said. 'It just doesn't add up. And I'm wondering if this is all about something else. Not reputation or money, but about manipulation. Perhaps it was all a game to him – manipulating people and situations.'

17

Garðar sat opposite Daði Sigurðsson in interview room fourteen. Daði was a skinny man with a pale complexion. He sat in a hunched posture, as if he was trying to disappear. It came as a surprise to Garðar to see just how insecure he was, considering the man's business reputation. He had expected a mogul like this to be arrogant and self-assured, but Daði was anything but. He had reacted badly to being brought in for questioning, and had done his best since to stick to the story that he and Óttar had barely been in touch since they were small boys in the town of Hafnarfjörður.

'We found documents relating to Óttar's offshore companies, as well as an agreement between you two about you fronting his companies here and overseas in return for a percentage of the revenue. So starting out by telling us lies about your relationship with Óttar doesn't look good for you,' Garðar told him.

Elín was at his side in the interview room, and added that they had only made a dent in the documents, but the extent of Óttar and Daði's activities through these companies already appeared to be substantial – they could see they'd acquired businesses in Iceland, for example.

Daði continued to slump deeper in his chair and mumbled his reply: 'I'm sorry, OK. I should have told you from the off, but I promised Óttar that I'd take this secret to the grave with me. That was part of our agreement. And, anyway, there's nothing illegal about buying companies in Iceland. We haven't done anything wrong. He just didn't want to be publicly connected to all this. He said it would be better to do things this way. He was just helping me to get established, and building up a pension pot of his own in the process, that's all.'

Elín seemed to have difficulty suppressing a derisive snort. She took a deep breath and a sip of coffee.

'Where were you on the evening of Óttar's death?' Garðar said abruptly, trying to catch Daði off guard.

'You don't think I had anything to do with it?' he replied, sitting up straight for the first time. 'What would I gain from that?'

'You're free of Óttar, and now it's just you who's sitting on all these assets,' Garðar said, slapping a hand on the bundle of documents.

'No, no. The agreement is very clear on that. It says if anything happens to Óttar, it all goes to his mother and sister. Once he's dead, I get nothing out of this.'

'Did you quarrel over business?' Garðar pressed. 'Could he have had other ideas about how the arrangement continued? Maybe he was intending to dump you?'

'He couldn't have done that without the whole thing becoming public,' Daði replied. 'You clearly haven't looked through these documents in any detail.'

He sat up even straighter, his self-assurance returning as he realised he had the upper hand for a moment.

'That doesn't mean anything. Óttar could have decided to go public and come clean. That wouldn't have been good for you.'

'Come clean?' Daði said with a yelp of laughter. 'You clearly didn't know Óttar.'

'So where were you the evening Óttar was murdered?'

'At home. In front of the TV. I binge-watched the whole *Chernobyl* series.'

'Is there anyone who can confirm that?'

'I've no idea. Some of my neighbours might have seen me. I live alone, except when my son is with me, but he wasn't that night ... Do I need to call a lawyer?'

'You can do that if you feel you need to, but we just want to talk to you about these business arrangements. We have some more questions, if that's all right with you...?'

'Yes. Sure.'

Garðar looked at Elín, and she took over, as planned. She started by asking if Óttar had been aware of rumours about a new leak of information concerning offshore holdings.

'Yes, I had a conversation with a journalist who said he was working on an article about it. He asked me loads of questions but didn't seem to have connected Óttar to any of it. After the Panama Papers, and taking into account how badly it came across in the media for some people when they tried to deny everything, I thought it best to be truthful ... for the most part. I didn't mention Óttar's involvement in my holdings. Óttar and I met and spoke about it all, and we agreed that none of the possible revelations could lead back to him.'

Elín gave him a piercing look. 'You've acquired a substantial number of companies here in Iceland through these offshore holdings. While he worked for the government, did Óttar have any say in how these companies were sold – I mean how your offers were accepted and not others'? And could there be someone out there who has a grievance against Óttar because they found out he was behind these sales? It could be a reason for killing him, couldn't it?' Elín paused for a second. 'Do you know of anyone who would have wanted him dead?'

'It goes without saying that he wasn't called The Panther for no reason. He is ... sorry, he *was* smart and eloquent. He was the Teflon guy that nothing ever stuck to. He was well liked and always found ways to make sure "good solutions" went to the right people. I mean, he had half the country rooting for him at one point. People sought out his opinions – because he was widely respected. But I don't think you'll find anything that links him directly to the decisions to sell those companies to me. I'd say those who took those decisions had no idea that he was pulling their strings. He had a talent for that – always did. And nobody knew about the connection between us. We never let ourselves be seen together and kept our dealings very discreet.'

'You were childhood friends, weren't you?'

'You could say that. We got to know each other in Hafnarfjörður when we were about seven. But a few years later my family moved to Akranes, so we lost touch. That kind of acquaintance isn't much of a basis for a conspiracy theory, is it? But he got in touch with me again when we were in high school. Most people don't know about this. That's just how he wanted it. I was at Breiðholt College and he was at the Commercial College. We used to meet occasionally and drive out into the countryside to talk about our dreams for the future. We both longed to be successful – to earn money and respect. It was what we had in common. You probably don't know, but Óttar's voice was unbelievably enchanting. Sometimes I'd just close my eyes and listen to him expound on all our dreams for the future. If I close my eyes now, I can still hear it.'

Daði was wrong – Garðar did remember the persuasive quality of Óttar's voice and the gravity that had been a feature of his personality.

'How come you ended up in business together?' Garðar asked.

'He went to Minnesota to study. I decided to go for business administration at the University of Iceland. We used to write to each other now and again, and kept those dreams of ours alive. He really inspired me. I'm not sure I would have finished my degree if he hadn't sent me those letters telling me how we could make something of ourselves when our studies were over. Then, when he came home, we started to talk things over again and started to push things in the right direction. He'd brought some money back with him from the States – said he'd been lucky over there.'

'You know, we've had conversations with members of Óttar's family,' Garðar said, 'and they've not mentioned your friendship with him once.'

Daði sighed and examined his fingertips, hunching forward and appearing to shrink into his chair once more.

'We both had very few friends. He'd go out with some of the Commercial College kids. But I had no friends at all while I was at college. I was a total loner. He used to say it was best to keep it to ourselves that we knew each other, that it could become common knowledge sometime later, when we had hit our targets. I followed his advice. I don't know why. I was just pleased that he shared his dreams with me.'

Daði had become distant now, as if recalling his childhood and school years was difficult for him.

'You say he didn't have many friends. How about when you were younger, at school? Did he have a difficult time? Socially, I mean.'

'Not to begin with, but just before we moved to Akranes, he was starting to be more reserved. His mother was very strict with him, and he was at home a lot or out on his own. Don't get me wrong, he had lots of pals and was a bit of a joker, but nobody got close to him. That's what I meant by him having few friends.' Daði paused, reached for the jug of water on the table and topped up his glass. 'I was bullied quite a bit before I got to know Óttar. After, nobody dared touch me, not while he was around. He came across as so confident, he could scare off the bullies with just a glance. But then I went to a new school in Akranes and it all started again. I was skinny and pretty puny, so making me cry was a game for the other kids. When I got into high school, I decided to keep to myself, went to my classes, kept my head down. That worked. I was left alone, but at the same time, I didn't make any friends.'

Garðar decided that Daði's difficulties making friends weren't exactly relevant to the investigation, and that they'd had enough information out of him for the moment. He glanced at Elín and asked if she had any further questions.

'Not right now. But I'll need to speak to you again when I've taken a closer look through all your business affairs, Daði. You're not about to leave the country, are you?'

'No. And I'll gladly answer all your questions if it helps you find Óttar's murderer. I want you to find out who killed him. Óttar was really my only friend and I was fond of him.'

'I'll still have to ask your neighbours to confirm that you were at home on Wednesday evening last week,' Garðar said. 'I also need to check your phone log for that evening. Did you hear anything from Óttar the day he was murdered?'

'No. We spoke after I had that conversation with the journalist about possible revelations. We decided that we'd be in touch if either of us heard anything relevant to us. So it must be around three weeks since we last spoke.'

'I find that hard to believe, considering the extent of your business together,' Garðar said, a sharp edge to his voice.

This appeared to sting Daði, as he snapped back, 'It's just what happens when people do business together secretly. They try to keep it as quiet as possible. We rarely spoke and always tried to meet out of town somewhere if we had something to discuss. If you check the call logs, you'll see that there were only a few very short calls between us, and those were simply to decide where to meet in person.'

Garðar stared at him for a moment. Then thanked him for coming, asking him to stay close to home as they would need to speak to him again before long.

'Of course. It's best to call this,' Daði said, handing Garðar a business card and seeming to have calmed down again. 'I always answer right away on that number.'

When Garðar and Elín returned to the incident room, the others looked up expectantly.

'Does he look like a prospect?' Unnar asked, a hopeful glint in his eye. 'Are you keeping him in custody?' Garðar could see in his team's faces the hope that they were a step closer to finding their perpetrator.

'Unfortunately, I don't think we have strong enough grounds to hold him,' Garðar said. 'They were certainly in closer contact than the paperwork would indicate, and even their close family members knew nothing about their relationship. But Elín and I agree that he had no convincing motive for murdering his business partner. We'll know more when we have a legal opinion on the validity of the agreement between them, so for the moment nothing's ruled out. We've released him, even though his alibi still needs to be confirmed. He says he was at home that evening, watching TV alone. It would be useful if one of you could call his neighbours and find out if anyone noticed him on Wednesday evening. Viktor, would you do that?'

'Yep. No problem. I'll check this evening which of his neighbours would be most likely to have seen him and I'll call around them in the morning. We can also check his internet usage and TV streaming – as that's undoubtedly connected to the internet as well.'

Garðar stared at him in incomprehension. 'Can you do that? God help us, there's no peace or privacy anywhere these days. But if it helps in this case, then I won't stand in your way. We're going to have to move fast though. And that goes for everyone.'

Garðar raised his voice a little and looked around the room to make sure he had the whole team's attention. 'Pressure from the media about this case is building up. It's been relatively easy to convince his family and colleagues that an investigation like this takes time, but the media don't care. They just see something juicy that they want to milk to death. I suppose it's understandable this time, as it's almost unheard of for a man in his position to be a murder victim, and we shouldn't forget that he was a prominent figure in the media only a few years ago, so some journalists will know him personally. I gather his mother and sister aren't answering calls from numbers they don't recognise because they're being hounded by hacks. So for their sake, and ours, we need to make good progress, and soon. A trail such as this can go cold very quickly so we need to pull all these threads together. We've requested additional funding so we can allocate more manpower to this case, and that's being looked at favourably.' Garðar looked at each face in turn, hoping that he had managed to give his team the impetus they needed.

As they went back to their various tasks, he walked slowly into his office and allowed himself to collapse into his chair. This was turning out to be one of the toughest cases Garðar had even taken on. Óttar had clearly lived a double life; one in which he was first a star pundit and then a civil servant, and another in which he was a big wheel in the investment machine, which he had been able to conceal successfully. Garðar was convinced that this dual existence was where the answers lay, and he decided that the focus in the coming days would be on a detailed search through all the documentation.

His thoughts turned to Sigurdís. She was very smart, but all the same, he felt that her observations during the investigation had been juvenile. He smiled to himself when he recalled what she had said about Óttar's laundry habits – as if that had any bearing on anything. But perhaps he was being unfair to her: she had found the safe in which he was sure the key to the whole mystery lay, after all. And then she and Unnar had found out the truth behind the transfers to the American bank. He was deeply fond of her and he never failed to shudder whenever he recalled how he and her father's colleagues had failed Sigurdís and her brother, let alone their mother.

Sigurdís's aunt, Halla, had spoken to him and his superior officer at the time, telling them that their colleague was beating his wife. Garðar had found it difficult to believe, but he had expected that his superior officer would at least look into the accusation. He had clearly decided not to. And then things ... well, things had turned out the way they'd turned out.

Garðar felt a stab of regret that he hadn't visited Sigrún, Sigurdís's mother, for a few months. He had visited her regularly to begin with. His wife, Gunnhildur, had also been a regular caller, bringing her home-cooked meals, but over time this had become gradually less frequent. He decided that he would have to pay her a visit when things were quieter. Garðar had never mentioned these visits to Sigurdís. He assumed she knew he paid them, but then again he had no idea of what kind of a relationship she now had with her mother.

He stood up and went to the door, but paused for a second, looking back into his office as if he'd forgotten something. Finally, he made his decision: he would let Sigurdís remain on the investigation team and carry out various assignments. He owed her that much.

✳ 18 ✳

AGNAR JÓNSSON

Daniel Christensen. I can't say how tired I am of that name. My name's Agnar Jónsson and I want to be Agnar Jónsson! But they wrecked that good name of mine. They didn't understand, and that old cow, Sigrún, didn't help matters. She went completely nuts and did nothing to support me. I tried to tell everyone that she had destroyed our home life. Destroyed my life. My relationship with the children. Destroyed everything with her moaning and belly-aching, poisoning everything around her. Completely mental she was. Of course I got angry sometimes. Who wouldn't? Surely the children will understand, now they're grown up. I just need a chance to explain. Einar must have seen my messages by now. Isn't the boy going to reply? It's Friday night already, dammit, and still no response!

Einar Hölluson. Hölluson! He doesn't even take my name for his patronymic. Halla was a snake in the grass, just like their mother. No doubt she's still pouring poison into their ears, telling them I was a bad man. I'm not that at all. It was an accident, and they have to understand that. It was an accident, because their mother was nuts, which was why everything got so out of hand that night. Anyone can lose their temper. They don't know what it was like living with someone as crazy as she was.

I'll send the boy another message. He must answer soon.

21.40
I would appreciate a reply, my boy. I never intended to hurt you or
your sister. Your mother simply wasn't in good mental health and
I was constantly trying to help her. She didn't want that. She
wanted to live in her own mad world, and that's how it happened.
It was just an accident. You must understand that.

No more beer. The boy must get back to me now. How can you
be so disrespectful to your own father, your own flesh and
blood? I was a respected police officer until she wrecked
everything. I want to go back to my homeland. I *will* go home.
They can't take away my origins. I'm an Icelander. We resist when
we feel we have been wronged!

I'll check on Dennis in the next room. He must have more
beer. He always has beer.

'Dennis, Dennis. *Kom nu*. Open up and give me a beer!'

'What's all the noise about, Daniel?'

'Give me a beer!'

'Yeah, yeah. Take it easy. I'll give you a cold one.'

'Take it easy? Don't you tell me to take it easy. Show me some
respect, you arsehole.'

That wretched boy can't talk to me like that.

'Sorry, Daniel. I was asleep. There are two beers and you can
have them both.'

'Grand. That's more like it.'

'There you go. Good night.'

I bid the lame idiot good night. He's a hopeless character who
does nothing but flatter people. I hate flattery. These Danes are
like that all the time. It's best if I get away from here. I've had
enough of the shit work and crap money. They treat me like a
pig here on the farm. It's time to take things into my own hands
and stop going with the flow, working for arseholes for peanuts.
I wasn't supposed to live like this. Arseholes. They're all

arseholes. The door of my room doesn't even shut properly. What a dump.

I'll message him again. He must respond, the lad. Shit, this old computer takes an age to get going. It'll be great to be home. In Iceland. Iceland! My homeland. The worst of it is that a bunch of reds were allowed to take over after the crisis. The place needs sorting out again.

He's answered. That took a while.

22.10
Accident? How can breaking one child's skull and the other's leg be an accident?

22.12
Do you think I meant to hurt you? Has Halla been telling you that? Be wary of her. She lies and spreads poison all around her. You're my children. I love you both.

22.14
I genuinely love you. You have to believe me and give me an opportunity to explain how your mother poisoned my mind. Is she still mental? Too crazy to look after her children? I tried to tell her, all those years. In the end, I snapped. Anyone who had to live with that for years on end would do the same.

22.17
Are you prepared to meet? I can explain everything. Everything will become clear if I can get home and speak to you directly.

22.18
Einar?
Aren't you going to answer me?

22.21
Answer your father, Einar!

22.22
Are you becoming like your mother?
Crazy?

22.25
Answer me, boy!

22.25
We will meet again. I promise you that. Answer me, Einar.
Hölluson? Is this some kind of a joke? How can any man take some
old bag's name? Has Halla taken away your manhood?

That bloody boy. Cocky, just like his mother, and then silence. She often wouldn't even give me the time of day. He's got that from her. He doesn't have the strength of character to look himself in the eye any more than she did. He wouldn't have been like that if I'd brought him up. I'd have brought him up to be a man. It takes a man to raise a man! Now I need to get home and put things to rights. It's time to reclaim what's mine. Next pay day I'll buy myself a ticket. No, I'll get an advance. I'll ask for an advance, and go as soon as I can. This can't go on. Iceland. My beloved country. I'm coming home!

19

'I'm here,' Sigurdís called out as she pushed open the door of Halla's house, ready for a late breakfast.

Halla lived in a terrace on Háaleitisbraut with Einar and her husband, Gunnar, who she had got to know four years ago. He was a quiet, reliable character, and Sigurdís and Einar had become fond of him, not least because he was so good to Halla.

'In the kitchen,' Halla called back. 'The table's laid.'

Halla had certainly made an effort. Anyone would have thought that royalty were stopping by. But that's the way she was, one of those people who always went a step beyond what was expected. There was fresh-baked bread on the table, jam, butter, salmon, fruit, and a childhood favourite.

'That brings back sweet memories,' Sigurdís said. 'Crispbread, cheese and pink caviar in a tube. I can't wait.'

'Well, what are you waiting for?' asked Gunnar as he came into the kitchen. 'Looks like we have the same taste,' he added with a smile, giving Sigurdís a kiss on the cheek.

'You're looking after yourself, aren't you, Sigurdís?' Halla asked, a concerned look on her face.

'Why? Do I look a bit peaky?'

'No, sweetheart, you look just fine, as always. I just worry about you in that stressful job. You know you can always come to us and recharge your batteries.'

'Whoo-hoo, a feast!' Einar whooped as he came into the kitchen, his hair wet and wrapped in the green dressing gown that Sigurdís had given him at Christmas. He had laughed at the time, telling her that he was relieved she was giving him old-man stuff as presents.

'Wow, that looks good on you,' Sigurdís said.

'And there's caviar all over your face,' Einar laughed.

As they wolfed down the food, Gunnar told them hunting tales. He hunted ptarmigan, reindeer and all sorts. Sigurdís told him that it was something she could never do. Gunnar laughed, and said that someone had to pave the way to the freezer for those blessed animals.

Sigurdís grinned at this. Then looked at her brother. 'Einar, are you tired?' she asked, catching his eye. She'd noticed that her brother seemed preoccupied while Gunnar was speaking.

'Yes, to be honest. I was at work yesterday and there was a group that we thought were never going to leave. It took forever to clear up and it was one-thirty by the time I got home,' he replied. 'So I'm a bit shattered. When do you need to be off?'

'In half an hour.'

Einar suggested that when they'd finish eating they should sort out Netflix for her, setting up an account in her name. 'We can do it on the computer in my room,' he said.

'Ach. I'm not bursting with energy right now. Can't we do it some other time?' Sigurdís wheedled.

'Later, later, says the lazy man,' Einar said. 'Isn't that what you taught me?'

'I have taught you well, my boy,' Sigurdís intoned in a deep voice, and laughed.

Upon entering Einar's room, he shut the door behind them then turned and gave Sigurdís a worried look.

'He made contact again yesterday,' he said in a low voice. 'Said that everything he did to us was an accident.'

'He said what…?' Sigurdís dropped down on the bed, suddenly feeling weak.

'I can't tell you how bad I felt reading his message,' Einar went on. 'I wasn't angry – more ... drained. I suppose that all along I had hoped deep inside that the truth wasn't really as bad as I'd been told. So it's like I've really seen the truth. When I read what he was saying, I realised that he's out of his mind. And I ... now, don't lose it when I tell you, but I replied.'

She opened her mouth to speak, and was ready to stand up, but he put out his hand.

'Wait, don't say anything yet. I just couldn't stop my fingers from typing after I read what he had written about it all being an accident. I ... I asked how he could say that breaking his son's head and his daughter's leg was accidental. Like I said, I wasn't angry. It just felt like being in some surreal drama. It felt like it wasn't me, but someone else, who had to tell that man these things.'

'Oh, Einar, love, why didn't you call me straight away? You know you can call or come over to my place whenever you like.'

'It was all so unreal. I came home as if I'd been hypnotised. I sent him a message just before the rush at work started. I read through all the responses he sent while I sat in the car after my shift. Sigurdís, I didn't sleep a wink last night. Just lay under the duvet and cried. I don't know what came over me, answering him like that. My curiosity got the better of me, I suppose. But now I'm worried I've woken a monster.'

'What do you mean, Einar, "all the responses"? Did he reply to you then? Can I see?'

'Reply? Just a bit. I got a whole flood of insane abuse.'

'Show me.'

Einar unlocked his phone and handed it over with a big sigh.

Sigurdís read through the messages with mounting horror.

'He's coming, Sigurdís,' Einar said. 'You see him say it? I should never have replied to him.'

Sigurdís put her arms around her brother.

'It's not your fault,' she said fondly. 'None of this is your fault. He's a violent man and if he hadn't used Facebook, then he would have found some other way to approach us. He's clearly already decided to come back to Iceland and make contact one way or another. You did well, showing him that there's no red carpet waiting for him here.'

Einar looked into his sister's eyes. 'Team?'

Sigurdís hugged him again. 'Of course we're a team,' she whispered.

There was a light tap at the door and Halla put her head around it.

'Lovely to see you two so close. Would you like anything more to eat before you go back to work, Sigurdís?'

'No, thanks. I'm full. That was wonderful, as always.'

She glanced at Einar and added that she would call him in the evening so he could finish setting up Netflix for her. 'We can get ourselves a pizza and watch a film or something.'

'Let's do that. Hope it goes well at work and say hello to Garðar. Mum said he still calls in to see her sometimes, but she hasn't seen him for a few months.'

Sigurdís stopped on her way to the door. She was taken aback. 'Garðar still goes to see her?'

'Yes, he calls in and chats with her.'

Sigurdís felt the heat rise in her cheeks, and wondered why Garðar had never mentioned it to her.

'That's so good of him,' she said through a forced smile as a way of ending the conversation.

Once Halla had gone, Sigurdís turned to Einar and told him that he shouldn't worry himself. She would mention the old man's messages to Garðar and ask him to check up on him.

'I'll speak to you later,' she said, and gave him another forced smile.

* 20 *

Unnar was already at the station when Sigurdís arrived at a quarter to eleven.

'Is Garðar in his office?' she asked him, feeling a bit anxious about their conversation of the night before.

'Yes, he's in there and making heavy weather of it. I reckon he's frustrated about our lack of progress on this case, and the media won't leave him alone. But we're making a push on the documents from the safe today. Elín is working out an overview of this whole tangle of financial connections so she's going to need our help tying up the loose ends and filling in the gaps. She's really plunged into this and I don't think she's slept, just deep in all this stuff day and night. It must be wonderful for her and her husband to have Óttar in bed with them!' Then he suddenly seemed to realise how inappropriate it was to be making a joke of this, flushed slightly and looked away.

'That would make an interesting love triangle,' Sigurdís said, throwing him a lifeline, and they both laughed awkwardly. 'One thing I was wondering,' she went on. 'Have Óttar's movements been tracked through his phone?'

'We're looking into that with the network provider. But it's not as easy as it was to track someone's whereabouts through their phone – there are some new strict conditions you have to meet. A few years ago it was no problem to check what numbers were in a particular area at a given time. But now the data protection rules say we can't retrieve that information unless we have good reason to have someone under suspicion. And we can only get broad authorisation in the case of a missing person. I heard Garðar arguing with the legal department about it. But the law is the law, so we have to take a roundabout route these days. It's all to ensure people's data stays secure, I suppose.'

'It's understandable, now that everything we do can be tracked through some satellite,' Sigurdís said.

Elín had entered the room so quietly, Sigurdís jumped a bit when she spoke behind her, telling them Garðar wanted everyone working on the case to gather in the meeting room in a few minutes.

As they filed into the room and saw Elín sitting behind the stack of documents, ready to give them her overview, there was a murmur of anticipation about what she might have found there.

'Óttar went to great lengths to hide his financial shenanigans,' Elín began as she leafed through the documents from the safe. 'I've rarely seen anything like it. If he hadn't been murdered, we'd probably never have known a thing about what he was up to. But I think I've managed to put together a pattern.'

Going back to the years prior to the financial crisis, Elín told them how Óttar had begun acquiring substantial assets though his tax-haven entities, his old friend Daði Sigurðsson acting as front man so Óttar's name was connected to none of these purchases. Óttar appeared to have made all the investment decisions, however, and the indications were that he had based these on information that wasn't publicly available. It seemed to Elín that he had indirectly influenced the decision to sell four state-owned assets at a time when the market was still uncertain and those companies were therefore sold off cheaply.

'One of them ended up in Daði's hands, as I have explained before. And this was at the same time as Óttar was lobbying for the introduction of greater transparency in the disposal of state assets. I also found a paper trail showing that when he was a private consultant, before taking the position at the ministry, he worked for several companies that subsequently got into trouble by being over-mortgaged or over-geared – basically had a lot of debt. And while he was in the media spotlight talking about corruption, those companies ended up in his hands, through his friend Daði. So, I wouldn't be surprised if there were a few people who held a grudge against Daði.'

'Could anyone have found out that Óttar was behind all this?' Sigurdís asked.

'I see no indication that anyone knew of all this,' Elín replied. 'At least, there's nothing to that effect in the documents I have seen. That's something for you to figure out, I guess.'

'Thank you, Elín,' said Garðar. 'That was very useful. It proves what we suspected. Now, I have some news: Daði has been in touch with me this morning. He promised he would if he was tipped off about the media getting hold of any of this information. And it appears they have. He's been told that the impending exposé that Elín told us about previously will reveal the connection between him and Óttar.'

'Well there you go, then,' Elín said.

'There we go, what?' Unnar asked.

'We have a motive for Óttar's murder,' Elín said shortly. 'But, hey, I'm just in financial crime. What do I know?'

Unnar frowned. Sigurdís wondered if he, like herself, wasn't convinced about this angle on the investigation; it discounted all the information they'd found out about Óttar's time in the US. 'What do you think, Garðar?' Unnar said. 'Do you want me to try and track down what's happening with the exposé, and what exactly it will say about Óttar?'

'No, Elín and I will work on it. I want you to continue talking to Daði's neighbours. We ought to tie that up, as we can't completely exclude him yet as a suspect.'

03.05.1995

I'm in love. In love. We're going to have a great life together. Mr Sweet says such lovely things about our future. A future full of happiness. I'm counting the days until we can live together. I've had enough of this place. I have to get out of here. To him. To find peace. With him. He says our souls will become one.

✳ 21 ✳

Sigurdís sat at her desk and tried to piece together in her mind all the information Elín had brought them at the meeting. She could sense that she was developing an obsession with this case, but she wasn't as convinced as most of the others were that it was linked to Óttar's financial dealings. It wasn't as if she could go to Garðar and tell him so, though, simply because she had a gut feeling about it. It would be almost worth doing it, just to see the expression on his face, she thought with a smile. On the other hand, she had to consider the possibility that she was on the wrong track. If she was to be a real detective, then she would have to build a case that would withstand scrutiny, and not base it on intuition.

She decided to toe the line, and start on the task she'd been assigned at the end of the meeting – to chase after the information that had been leaked, and find out wherever it might have ended up.

Who could have seen this stuff? Sigurdís thought to herself, certain that they would have to find the news outlet who was going to publish the exposé and squeeze out of them which journalist had been in touch with Daði.

But after a few minutes, she found she was having a hard time focusing on her work. It was because the conversation with Einar that morning was still at the forefront of her mind. That wretched loser had been persecuting Einar. She'd seen the messages. The poor boy had replied on impulse. She couldn't blame him for doing it. She could feel the rage building up inside her as she thought about it. *I'll have to talk to Mum,* she thought. *I need to know more about that man and the kind of behaviour she had to put up with all those years. I need a better idea of what to expect from him.*

She felt her stomach turn with fear and anger. She needed to protect her brother. He'd already suffered enough. She couldn't just do nothing now that her father had been harassing him. Although they were busy with a major murder investigation, she would have to speak to Garðar about the old man's threat to come home. She wouldn't be able to concentrate until she had done that.

She sighed and made her way over to Garðar's office, tapped at his door and opened it. He was standing by the open window, with his left hand outside as a trail of smoke dribbled from the corner of his mouth.

'Shut the door, would you, Sigurdís? I've relapsed ... And lock it so nobody comes in. I need to finish this cigarette,' Garðar said mournfully. 'I was about to call everyone together – we've just had the post-mortem results.'

'Anything new?' Sigurdís asked.

'Not really. The initial assessment seems to have got it right. The cause of death was a bleed on the brain due to a heavy blow. He seems to have been lying on the beach for a while, still alive and possibly conscious, without being able to move – the inflammation that accompanies the bleeding would have left him largely paralysed. And he would have died slowly. There's bruising in a couple of places, possibly from being kicked when he was on the ground. The bleeding under the skin indicates that these injuries must have occurred around the same time as he received the blow to the head. So, all in all, nothing we didn't already know.'

Sigurdís could see that even though it wasn't long since

Óttar's body had been found, this investigation was taking its toll on Garðar. She wasn't sure if she ought to be adding her own troubles to his burden, so she stood there for a moment, heavy in her own thoughts. It was as time slowed down while she anguished about what to say next.

'Something on your mind, Sigurdís?' Garðar said delicately. 'Your eyebrows always give you away.'

'I ... well. Sorry, but this doesn't make things here any better...' She fell silent.

When she didn't continue, Garðar spoke up.

'Although we work together, Sigurdís, we have a lot of shared history and you're important to me. You can tell me what's on your mind. I know you don't let the small shit worry you, so this must be something big.'

'The old man got in touch with Einar last night,' she blurted out.

She saw the look on Garðar's face go from paternal concern to straight-out fury.

'He doesn't seem to want to be told, does he?' he spat. 'How did he get hold of Einar? I know he's not in the country. I keep tabs on him.'

'On Facebook Messenger, under a Danish name. And ... well, unfortunately, Einar replied,' Sigurdís said, choking back a sob. 'And ... he said he's coming home.'

Garðar clenched his fists. 'Always the same self-centred narcissist. I'll never forgive myself for not acting back then. If only we'd had a better understanding of domestic violence. We handled all this so terribly – we just had no understanding how serious things were.'

Sigurdís couldn't respond. She had no idea what to say. She had heard this speech before and had said her piece multiple times. Now she just wanted to keep the focus on Einar's safety and wellbeing.

'Fortunately, things have changed within the force and the commissioner's policy on this is crystal clear,' he continued heavily.

'Can we please just focus on the matter on hand,' said Sigurdís, impatient now. 'The bastard is threatening to return and is planning God knows what.'

Garðar stubbed his cigarette out on the window sill outside before nodding in agreement. 'Would you ask Einar to send me the messages and the name he used? I'll look into it. I can at least try to keep him away from you.'

'Thank you. And please keep me updated so I can be prepared, and so I can warn Einar and Halla too.'

There was a depth of sympathy in Garðar's eyes now. 'And your mother? Will you tell her, or shall I?'

Her mother had either been in a daze or sedated ever since it had all happened. And Sigurdís's emotions towards her were thoroughly conflicted. There were days when she couldn't find it in her heart to forgive her – for saying nothing, for not screaming, for keeping everything hidden, for doing nothing and allowing things to go so far, for letting that arsehole injure her and Einar. On other days Sigurdís sympathised deeply with her as the victim of long-term domestic abuse.

She sighed. 'It's probably best if you tell her. I know you see her now and again.'

Garðar went over to the window, took out the red packet, extracted another cigarette and lit it with a match.

'Do you get through to her when you see her?' he asked, staring at the smoke as it glided out of the window with a slow, irregular motion. 'Sometimes I'm not sure how much she hears when I speak to her. Mostly we don't say anything,' he continued, as if speaking to himself now. 'Or I talk and she listens ... at least I think she's listening. Then she fetches some water, or makes coffee. Sometimes she gets a photo album and just holds it in her hands. When I ask if she's going to show me the pictures, she shakes her head and says that these are her pictures and she's the only one who looks at them.'

Sigurdís stared at him in astonishment. Her mother had never once taken out any photo albums on the few occasions she had visited her. She had only stared at her with a mournful look. Occasionally Sigurdís noticed a shadow of a smile, or some kind of attempt at one, when she told her about her life and Einar's, and what the two of them were up to. No, Sigurdís really wasn't sure she was up to having a conversation with her mother about her father's reappearance in their lives.

'She's not exactly talkative with me either,' she said. 'And it can be a bit uncomfortable to be around her, although I admit that I don't make a habit of it. I would be grateful if you could give her the news. I'm not sure it's something I can talk about to her without some upset being involved, and we both know it's best to avoid that with her.'

She saw a slight smile break onto Garðar's face, but then it vanished. He nodded to the door.

'Go on. We have a murder to solve, remember? And I need to smoke on the sly, and there's nothing sly about it if you're here.'

Sigurdís let out a short laugh, shaking her head as she shut the door behind her.

Sigurdís hadn't been sitting at her desk for long when she felt the need to speak to her mother surging through her. It was a need she hadn't felt in a long time, and was clearly prompted by her conversation with Garðar. She was having even more of a hard time concentrating on her work now than before her conversation with him. She looked around the quiet room, stood up and slipped out, hoping she hadn't been noticed. She didn't want to risk Unnar asking where she was going and having to lie to him.

Even though the sun was high in the sky, the high-rise at Hátún had a gloomy look to it. Social services had got her mother an apartment there and she'd been living there for the past decade or so. Sigurdís felt the knot in her belly tighten as she looked up at the building and found her mother's balcony. She took a deep breath while counting to four, held her breath while counting to six and then exhaled slowly. This type of breathing usually helped her calm her inner turmoil. There was a calm breeze blowing around the tall buildings and she felt a sudden chill as she walked to the door, pushing it open and stepping into the untidy lobby. Newspapers lay in stacks and the names on most of the mail boxes had either been torn off or scratched out. She found the button for flat 6-F. It was stuck, but popped up as Sigurdís pressed it.

After a moment a feeble 'hello?' came from the speaker.

'It's me. Sigurdís.'

'Sigurdís?' the weak voice replied, before she heard the buzz of the door being unlocked.

The hallway of her mother's flat was narrow. A single pair of shoes sat on a pale wooden rack. The flat's walls were bare, apart from a mirror in the hall and a picture of Sigurdís and Einar that Halla had given their mother many years ago. The little kitchen was fitted out in old-fashioned oak-style cupboards, and on the counter were an empty glass and a cloth, folded next to the sink. The place was small and bright. There were few personal items, the furniture was old and the place smelled of coffee and stale air. The curtains were of different lengths and their colours didn't go with anything else in the room.

'How are you?' she asked her mother, who stood staring at her with a look of astonishment on her face.

The door was still open and Sigurdís wasn't sure if her mother was pleased to see her, or if she was waiting for her to change her mind and hurry back out – as she had done so often before.

'I'm ... I'm fine,' she said, finally closing the door. 'I don't have much to offer you, but I cooked some fish cakes for lunch, if you're hungry. You look very thin. Maybe you should be eating better.'

Sigurdís felt the blood rush to her cheeks and wanted to yell back that it was too late in the day to be having concerns about her health. Instead, she took a deep breath and replied that she wouldn't mind a cup of coffee. She thought brewing the coffee would give both of them an opportunity to collect themselves.

The coffee was strong and her mother served it to her in an old mug with a logo of a bank brand that had, many years ago, merged with one of the now-failed ones. They sat in silence for a long while, the hot mugs clasped in their hands. Sigurdís could feel her mother's gaze. She needed to take another deep breath.

It had been a long time since she had needed to take quite so many deep breaths. It would take days for her to wind down after this. It was just as well that these visits were rare, for the sake of her health.

She returned her mother's gaze, and she didn't look away, but continued to stare as if in a daze. She looked older. Her hair was grey and untidy, and it looked as if she had cut it herself. All the same, Sigurdís saw the remnants of a pretty face behind the drabness. She was dressed in thin tracksuit bottoms and a pink T-shirt. It seemed to her that her mother had shrunk, looking smaller and thinner. But it was still clear that Sigurdís and her mother were physically alike. Her mother held a single sheet of kitchen roll in one hand, as if waiting for Sigurdís to spill some coffee. If only she had always been so alert, she thought resentfully.

After sitting a while in awkward silence, Sigurdís decided to be direct. It was best not to dance around the reason she had called on her mother without notice.

'I'll get straight to the point. Your former husband has contacted Einar.'

'Who?' her mother asked, her expression unchanged.

'Do you have many former husbands?' Sigurdís snapped. 'The arsehole who almost killed Einar while you watched.'

She immediately regretted her sharp tone. Deep down she knew why she had come – it was an opportunity to berate the woman who had allowed the man she had married to beat both her and the children. Sigurdís wanted to see some expression, some kind of indication of regret, anger – or just some kind of emotion. But there was nothing. Her mother sat with the same sorrowful look on her face, as always, and said nothing.

'He's threatened to come back from Denmark, which is where he has been since he was released. Garðar said he'd tell you this, but I was passing by and decided to do it myself. I thought it was important that you were aware of it, although I don't know what you can do about it.'

Her mother's expression did not change at all; she just continued to stare.

'Is he here?' she asked at last.

Sigurdís didn't reply right away. She realised that she felt neither love nor hatred for her mother in that moment. She felt no emotion at all, apart from a tiny slither of sympathy.

'He only just contacted Einar a few days ago, and I don't suppose he went straight to the airport after. Garðar would have known. He keeps tabs on him, even though he's not really supposed to. He does it for me and Einar,' she said, then fell silent. 'Why did you marry him?' she asked suddenly, taking herself by surprise with her question. She had often wondered what could possibly have drawn her mother to her father, but she had never dared to ask. It was as if she didn't want to hear he could have some nice qualities about him.

Her mother's expression remained unchanged, although she shut her eyes for a moment before her lips moved. She spoke slowly.

'He was so handsome in his new police uniform. So handsome.'

She said no more.

Sigurdís decided to use the interrogation technique she had been taught, to stay silent, waiting for something more from the woman sitting opposite her, who she often felt was a stranger to her.

But nothing else was said in answer to her question. It was as if he had existed as nothing more than a ghost, determined to haunt them till the end of their days. Sigurdís sipped her coffee slowly, determined not to show how desperate she was to run out of there, and out of this awful silence – silence that stemmed from a thick, stale guilt. But Sigurdís was starting to realise it was not just her mother's guilt that lay over the room like a thick fog every time they met, but also her own. She felt guilty for not visiting her mother more often, and also for her anger towards her. Daughters are supposed to love their mothers unconditionally, but sometimes she wasn't sure if she felt any love for her mother at all.

After twenty minutes of silence and sipping coffee while her mother sat as still as a statue, Sigurdís decided that no more would be forthcoming from this visit. She stood up, feeling her mother's eyes on her.

'Well, I've given you the message and had a cup of coffee. I'd better be on my way.'

Her mother stood up and followed her into the hall. When Sigurdís turned in the doorway to say goodbye, she saw a broken person staring back at her. Her clothes hung on her frame and her expression was blank. But then, as if some invisible hand had poked her, she stood a bit straighter as she looked at her daughter in the doorway.

'Don't you worry, Sigurdís. Don't worry. Don't worry about a thing,' she repeated.

Sigurdís felt herself deflate. She wanted to tell her how sorry she was that the handsome man in his new uniform had turned out to be a wolf in sheep's clothing. She wanted to tell her mother that she had been a victim, just as she and Einar were. But she didn't have the energy to form those words. Instead she said that she would guard Einar with her life. She promised her mother she would do that. She noticed that the sheet of kitchen roll had vanished, except for a tiny corner protruding from her mother's clenched fist.

As Sigurdís went out into the passage, she thought she could hear someone banging on the wall, again and again. And she could hear her mother very clearly, repeating in a loud voice, 'He can't have them. He can't have them. He can't have them.'

❊ 23 ❊

'Óttar Karlsson's Offshore Billions'. Sigurdís was about to click on the link to the article when Elín came into the incident room.

'Hi. Reading up on what the media have to say about Óttar's offshore business?' she said looking at Sigurdís's screen. 'I can fill you in what we know so far, if you like?'

'Please do,' said Sigurdís and pointed to the seat next to her.

'As you know, we'd been waiting for something to turn up,' said Elín, sitting down, 'but couldn't find out which media outlet the info would come from. They were managing to keep it very close to their chests, and did a good job of it too. Anyway, now it's been published, it turns out this law firm in Panama, Sun & Senses, that we spotted in the documents from the safe, is at the heart of Óttar's dealings. As I said, my team have been waiting for a leak about Sun & Senses, and now all their business transactions have been made available on Wikileaks. I've spent all night going through them, and it turns out that Óttar has been a busy boy, making himself rich. He did it all away through these transfers via Panama. He really was a top-of-the-range rogue.'

Sigurdís laughed, guessing this was probably one of the worst things the honourable Elín could say out loud about another person.

'I can think of less polite words to describe him, now I know more about him from this investigation. I reckon any sympathy for him as a victim isn't going to last long.'

'You're probably right,' Elín replied, turning her mouth down. 'All the same, nobody has the right to deprive a person of life, and I'd have preferred to have seen him trying to explain himself in court than ending up dead on the beach.' She paused before continuing. 'Anyway, this leak is a treasure trove for the financial crimes unit – there's a long list of other names that fill in all the blanks in our picture of organised tax avoidance and money laundering. We've known it was taking place for some time but just couldn't get a grip on it all. And as far as Óttar's activities are concerned, the information is very extensive, and it's clear he was taking everyone he dealt with for an absolute fool. We can expect some political fireworks in the next few weeks, I think. It'll be interesting to see how the media are going to cover all this. They were the ones who put him on a pedestal to start with. It's a total clusterfuck.'

'Elín! The F-word!' Sigurdís laughed.

Elín's cheeks turned pink. 'Even though he was a scumbag,' she said, 'we still need to find the killer. All the same, I don't imagine there will be as many well-wishers at his funeral as there would have been before all this came to light.'

'I hear you've seen the latest news,' Garðar said, coming into the room. 'I've been at a meeting with the Minister of Justice and some officials. They're adamant that we continue with the investigation, but we're not getting any additional support from that financial-crime unit, as they'll be using all their manpower working on this new leak and what's being revealed. Elín, I insisted that you remain part of this investigation, and that was agreed – on the condition that you keep financial crime updated on your findings, as Óttar's sticky fingers are all over these papers.'

This was greeted with nods all round the room.

'The good news in all this is that we can be fairly sure someone had a good reason for wanting to bump him off,'

Garðar continued. 'I'd like you, Elín, to go through the documentation again, carefully, and provide me with a list of all the companies he had bought, and especially those that could have led to a grudge against him.'

Garðar had obviously put up a good fight for their team with the minister, as he was also able to inform them that he'd had the go-ahead to ask for support on the investigation from their colleagues in Norway. He spoke fast and it was clear he wanted to keep things moving at a fast pace, but before leaving the room, he asked Sigurdís to walk with him over to his office.

She felt the urgency in the air as she half ran after Garðar as he paced towards his office. His words seem to have created urgent chatter and fast movements among the team.

She shut the door behind her while Garðar took a red cigarette packet from his pocket.

'I'm going to tell you something now, Sigurdís – but you mustn't pass it on to anyone, or ask how I found out about it. It may be ethically defensible, but not legally, I think.'

He paused, giving her a hard look. She nodded briskly in assent.

'OK, good. Your father tried to book a flight to Iceland last night, but his credit card was declined.'

'Serves him right,' Sigurdís said.

'Yes. It's probably sunk his travel plans for the moment. But knowing him as well as I do, it'll just get him fired up. We have to hope he doesn't hurt anyone trying to get his hands on the money he needs. He won't let this stop him, I'm sure. According to my information, he tried the card a dozen times, and then called the booking staff and gave them an earful. If he comes here, then I'd be concerned about his actions, as he doesn't seem to think there's anything wrong in what he's doing. He's always seen himself as the victim in all this, so everything he does he thinks is completely justifiable.'

The reality of what was happening hit Sigurdís like a slap across the face. The room seemed to be closing in on her and she fell back against the wall behind her, sliding slowly down it until she was sitting on the floor.

Garðar crushed out his cigarette against the window ledge outside, stowed the stub away in a matchbox and sat down on a chair facing her.

'He won't get a chance to lay a finger on you,' he said, leaning forward and trying to give her a smile. 'I promise you that. But we keep this between the two of us until we know more. We're keeping a close eye on him.'

'Thank you, Garðar. You promise to let me know what happens? Keeping anything back isn't going to do me any favours. Keeping secrets won't do anyone any good at this stage.'

'I promise, Sigurdís.'

A weighty silence filled the office.

'What a mess,' Garðar said, finally breaking it. 'If you think about it, they are pretty similar, Óttar and Agnar. These aren't people who can keep themselves in check like the rest of us do. Both of them are completely blind to what's right and wrong and what effects their actions have. They've just gone about things in different ways. They both managed to play leading roles for a while, but people like that always get found out in the end.'

Sigurdís managed to stand up now, even though she felt shaky on her legs. She thanked Garðar then excused herself and rushed to the nearest toilet, where she threw up her breakfast.

✱ 24 ✱

Óttar Karlsson's dead. And not before time! thought Guðmundur Kaldal Brjánsson as he looked in the mirror. *That man with his fancy ways and his swanky job. A smooth-tongued bastard and a scoundrel he was. Forgive me, Grandad, forgive me, Dad. It should never have been like this. I thought I'd been the one who screwed up, that I'd ruined the company you had built from the ground up, the company you created, spurred by the bitter poverty you'd always known, all so that I could have a good life. That thieving bastard is dead now. He got what he deserved. I just wish that I could have beaten him so thoroughly that he would have been unrecognisable when he got his final send-off. I would have wanted to see him suffer for longer, to see his face as I pummelled him with these fists. For Dad, for our family, for the legacy he snatched away. If only he'd not died so swiftly. He got to go far too easily. God, I hate him.*

'Justice at last. Justice!' he screamed, before he smashed the mirror with a blow from his clenched fist.

25

Dóra had managed to drag Sigurdís to the theatre. In fact, Sigurdís hadn't had much choice in the matter, as when her friend decided to apply the pressure, there was no way to say no to her. Dóra was a regular theatregoer, and at the end of every performance, as the audience thundered applause, she would invariably give way to tears, regardless of whether the performance had been wonderful or mediocre.

'You don't understand, Sigurdís,' she said as the show ended and she dabbed at her eyes. 'There are flesh-and-blood people up there who have been giving it everything for two hours. I can't not share their joy, and sometimes that means tears.'

Sigurdís simply saw it as a sign of her friend's inner goodness. 'You're just a much better person than the rest of us,' she laughed, and hugged her. 'Let's go and find coffee somewhere.'

'Coffee!' Dóra snorted. 'No chance. It's time for something stronger, and it's time for us to look at some cute guys. We'll try a bar and see if we can dust off our flirting skills. Well, mine, at any rate. You still have to start learning how to flirt.'

Sigurdís laughed again and promised Dóra that she would pay careful attention to her renowned tactics and take notes. Enjoying the evening sunshine, they strolled from the National Theatre up Klapparstígur until they reached their favourite bar, Ölstofan. Luck was on their side and they found an unoccupied table right away, next to a window overlooking the street. Sigurdís sat down on the red bench, making sure she had a good view of the room. She always found it uncomfortable to have her back to strangers. She needed to see around her, and to have potential escape routes scoped out. Dóra had no idea of these private plans, and happily took the chair facing her.

The place was busy, and Sigurdís thought she detected a strange tension in the air. Perhaps this wasn't surprising, considering there had been a furious response during the day to the latest Panama revelations, and the government's reaction had been a robust one, with significant funds already earmarked for the investigation. This time there was clearly no intention of allowing another administration to implode over an international leak. Photos of people being brought in for questioning relating to extensive tax evasion and money laundering had already begun to appear in the media, and politicians and commentators were climbing over each other to express their disgust over the findings.

Dóra ordered herself a Moscow Mule, and asked for a strong one. Sigurdís ordered her usual, a Diet Coke.

'You could do with a proper drink now and again,' Dóra told her.

'Too late to start now,' Sigurdís said. 'And I really need to bring my A game to work these days, and it's as well to have a clear head, just in case I get called in.'

'Are you getting involved as much as you'd like to?'

'Well, yes, sort of. More than I was when we last spoke. There's plenty to do and we're short-staffed. It's not often that we get handed a complex murder investigation that's also linked to a such a big financial exposé. The whole case is fascinating, and so multi-layered, it's really drawing me in – it makes me want to dig deeper into detective work.'

'Wow, Sigurdís Holmes, I like that,' Dóra giggled as she cast her eye around the room, like a hunter looking for prey. 'This whole thing is quite something, though. That Óttar was a hell of a player. From what I've seen today in the media and the response from people who worked with him, nobody had any idea about all this stuff. For real? I don't believe it's possible to have a totally separate life without at least some people knowing about it. I'm just not convinced. My parents on the other hand don't believe any of it. They both wanted to see him stand for parliament and were convinced that he was the leader this country needed.'

'You know, Dóra. The guy was known as The Panther, and from what I've seen, he deserved that nickname. He played his part very well. Most of us think people do their jobs honestly. The majority just don't expect this kind of thing from people we trust – they don't have the imagination to ever consider anything different. And what he did was so simply complex that nobody twigged.'

'Simply complex! What's that supposed to mean? Are you collecting bullshit buzzwords so that you can stand for parliament?' Dóra looked at her with a sneaky grin.

'Ha! What I mean is that sometimes the scam is so simple that you simply don't see it.'

'There's something in that. But, my darling, let's move on to serious stuff. Are you coming with us to New York? We've all booked our tickets and the only one left who hasn't confirmed is you. Do it, please.' Dóra looked at her gravely. 'It would do you good, and I'd love to enjoy the city with my best friend.'

The thought of getting into an aeroplane made Sigurdís instantly nauseous, and her palms were suddenly damp with sweat. But after what she'd just said about deceit, and all the sneaky business she had seen from Óttar, she decided she had to be honest with her oldest friend.

'I have a confession to make, Dóra. I'm absolutely terrified of flying. Just talking about it sets off a carousel of air-crash images in my head. I even start to smell the jet fuel. So I'm just not sure I'm an ideal travelling companion.'

Dóra didn't so much as flinch. 'There's plenty of time to do something about that before we go. I'll book you on a fear of flying course. And there are plenty of statistics I can get for you that show how safe flying is.' Dóra trotted all this out as if Sigurdís's problem was perfectly fixable.

Sigurdís immediately regretted telling Dóra all this, as her friend always slipped seamlessly into solution-seeking mode whenever a difficulty presented itself.

'I'm not sure it's that easy to overcome, because this isn't a logical fear, but more some kind of physical reaction to an un-controlled thought. In my head I know better, and I recognise that flying is safer than travelling by car, but the body goes its own ways and logic gets left behind.' She sighed. 'I don't know. It's a crazy set of feelings that I will probably never get over.'

'Hey, we live in times when practically everything has been researched and there's help waiting on every corner. We just need to want it.'

Dóra was about to continue, when Sigurdís's phone began to vibrate. She plucked it from her pocket and saw that Unnar was calling.

'Hi,' she said as they connected. 'Hold on a moment. I'm just going to jump outside so I can hear you better.'

Sigurdís was thankful that Unnar had provided her with some respite from Dóra's enthusiastically brandished magic wand. She mouthed a 'sorry' to her and squeezed out of the bar and on to the street outside.

Unnar apologised for interrupting her wild night on the town.

Sigurdís laughed. 'Well, let's say you're saving my bacon, because the fleshpots are pretty tempting and there's no telling how things could end up.'

'I just wanted to let you know there was a quick meeting just now where Elín gave us a list of everyone who could have felt trampled on by Óttar and Daði and we'll need to interview some of them tomorrow. It would be good to have you on board. We're about to sit down and divide up the list between us. Can you come in now?' Sigurdís felt the frustration rise inside her. Why hadn't she been asked to join the meeting? 'I'll be right there,' she said through clenched teeth before ending the call.

Dóra was already chatting to people at the next table when Sigurdís returned.

'Listen, Dóra darling,' she said, giving her an apologetic smile, 'there's a whole bunch of people we need to question tomorrow, and we need to prepare tonight so I'm going to have to leave you here.'

'OK, Sherlock. I'll sit here a while and finish my drink. We'll talk tomorrow.'

'Shift your flirtometer into overdrive and tell me what you get up to. Sometimes I have a need to live dangerously, even if it's only through you.'

Sigurdís kissed her friend goodbye then squeezed her way through the bar again, a bit more forcefully than earlier, still fuming about missing tonight's briefing. Even though she didn't believe in the direction the investigation was being taken, she still wanted to be there, have a seat at the table. Her instincts, though, were still pulling her in another direction. She hadn't been able to get Carla out of her mind, and decided she should push the issue and suggest that someone went over to the States to interview her and Stephen, face to face.

26

'So are things finally heating up?' Sigurdís asked as she dropped into a chair in the meeting room with her game face on.

Elín stood by the screen and had just begun to go over more details about the list she had produced from the data.

'As I outlined in the meeting earlier, the list extends to fifteen companies owned by Óttar through offshore entities. These are only the companies that Daði and Óttar wholly owned or in which they held a controlling share. We'll not take their other investments into account right away. Of these fifteen, there are four that attracted my interest. First of all, furniture manufacturer Stólar & Borð. This company ended up in Daði's and Óttar's hands at a time when Óttar was consulting for them. The company's founder is still alive and is in a nursing home. There has been some focus on his son and granddaughter, as they lost practically everything. The daughter managed to hold on to her home, but her father lost his. Next is a communications company called Núll. This expanded rapidly after 2000, and was heavily involved in leveraged takeovers. This was pretty reckless, in my opinion, but the reason I've included this one on the priority list is that the main owner fell flat on his face and blamed everyone but himself for how things worked out. We had complaints from him a few years ago about Daði's business methods, and there were certainly indications of a deep grudge there. The other two are investment companies that had a lot of assets, both here and abroad. These two cases are remarkable, and on closer inspection, they both survived the financial crash with strong portfolios, from which Daði and Óttar have made a lot of money. In my opinion, the assessments of their standing following the crash were dubious, which resulted in them being taken over. But once the dust had settled, both quickly got back into gear. This could have left some noses seriously out of joint. Personally, I can understand that. Any questions?'

Unnar put up his hand and coughed. 'The financial-crime division are seeing this stuff for the first time now, after these revelations from Panama. Óttar was murdered before all this became public knowledge. So we can't be certain that these people knew anything about Óttar's involvement?'

'We have confirmation that the media that worked on this with Wikileaks did contact some of these individuals before going public, to seek information from them. So that fits into our timeframe – it would've been *before* Óttar was killed,' Garðar said. 'However, we are yet to ascertain whether or not any of the journalists mentioned Óttar by name.'

Sigurdís was really beginning to wonder whether the investigation was on the right track. If it turned out that Óttar's name hadn't been mentioned by any journalists or reporters during their conversations with the former owners of these companies – and Elín, and even Daði himself, had mentioned several times that Daði and Óttar kept their relationship very well hidden – then why would these people have any motive to go after Óttar? In addition, she recalled that most murders are committed by someone close to the victim, and it was rare for business to be a motive.

'Garðar,' she began tentatively, 'have we ruled out the family connections or the links to America as part of this investigation?'

'What we have here is the most solid set of leads so far, Sigurdís. So we'll base our work on these. Do you have any reliable leads that point elsewhere?'

Sigurdís felt the heat in her cheeks, not because she felt it was right to rule out other options, but because Garðar's reply had been so abrupt. She could sense the irritation among the others too. She would have to take care to keep her feet on the ground if she intended to be taken seriously on this investigation. In reality she had no solid evidence to tell her the answer lay somewhere other than in these business dealings – nothing more than Carla's manner on the phone call, Stephen's appearance in Iceland, and her own intuition.

'No, I don't, and we haven't done any serious investigation in that direction. It's at your discretion, and it's undoubtedly right to check the business angle first,' she said.

Everyone stood up quietly and went to their workstations. Sigurdís felt the urge to disappear for a while. But she couldn't leave without telling Unnar how she felt about the investigation.

'They're totally anchored to this aspect of the investigation,' Sigurdís murmured to him in a low voice as they sat down at their desks. 'But I can't shake this feeling I have about it being more personal.'

Unnar gave her a sincere look then nodded to the coffee machine by the door. They poured themselves a cup each then headed outside to the carpark to drink it, where they found a spot the size of a postage stamp where the sun wasn't blocked by the building or the large, long fence surrounding the station's compound.

'As you could hear in the meeting, Sigurdís, I sympathise with you – I think we should be looking into other angles. But it's all about timing on an investigation like this. You have to find the right way to approach things and the right moment to do it. Irritating Garðar with it now is not going to help. So just wait for the time being, then bring it up again later, and in the meanwhile you can quietly strengthen your argument and be better prepared if needed.'

She knew he was right, but he hadn't been the one who spoke to Carla. There was something there, she was sure of it.

'You should have heard Carla's voice. The way she reacted to my questions, and particularly to the news of Óttar's death. And what about him having a son he kept quiet about? It all just makes me want to talk to her face to face.' She sighed and took a sip from her coffee before looking up at Unnar again. 'Maybe I should go over there and do exactly that?'

He looked at her in an astonishment, as if she had told him she was pregnant after visiting a solarium.

'Garðar would never approve of that, and also, you would need someone with you there. And after what was said in the meeting today, I just don't think Garðar and the rest of the team would see this lead as strong enough to warrant further investigation, and they certainly wouldn't think it's the basis for action as drastic as travelling to the USA.'

27

Unnar and Sigurdís had been assigned to interview Guðmundur Kaldal Brjánsson, who had been the owner of one of the companies on Elín's list. After numerous failed attempts to reach him by phone, they decided to visit his home. He was registered as living on Auðbrekka in Kópavogur, an old industrial street that had seen better days, with service companies and small industries leaving the area for more suitable premises on the outskirts of the capital. His building turned out to be a dilapidated two-storey industrial unit. There was no indication that any activity was taking place there, nor that anyone might be living in the building. In fact it looked derelict. They decided to walk around it to see if there were any signs of life. An old rusty van, held together by hope alone, was parked at the back.

'Wow. Can anything get passed as roadworthy these days? This one's rusting away,' Unnar said with a grin.

'Why so superficial, Unnar? Maybe it purrs like a cat the moment you turn the key? Looks aren't everything.'

Unnar looked across at her in mock admiration and placed a hand over his heart. 'Oh, such wisdom and depth.'

Sigurdís laughed. 'We should check if there's someone here,' she said. 'Let's knock on the door or pull the handle to see if it's open, there might be a flat upstairs.'

They knocked on a glass door at the back of the building and peered through it to see a floor space inside covered with junk.

There was no movement to be seen. Sigurdís took hold of the door handle. The door wasn't locked. It opened onto a hallway with three doors that led to the ground floor area and the stairs leading up to the next level.

'Who's there?' a hoarse voice called from above, and they heard heavy footsteps approaching the top of the staircase.

'We're from the police. We're looking for Guðmundur Kaldal Brjánsson,' Unnar called out in a stern voice.

A man appeared at the top of the stairs and came lurching down towards them, holding the handrail to support himself. He was so unsteady that Sigurdís half expected him to tumble forwards down the stairs. He was heavily built, dressed in a shirt and tie that had once been stylish but now looked shabby and creased. His shirt was untucked and was unbuttoned from halfway down his chest, so that his protruding belly seemed ready to escape and find itself somewhere else to live. It was clear he was very drunk and confused.

'What the fuck do you want?' he rasped.

'Are you Guðmundur Kaldal?' Unnar asked.

'Didn't I just say so, boy?'

'We have some questions to ask you.'

Guðmundur sighed and sank down onto the bottom step, leaning against the hand rail. 'About what?'

'Óttar Karlsson. You know him?'

'That bastard. He stole my company – my family legacy. Since then I've had to make do here, flat broke in a freezing-cold building that's infested with rats while my Núll ... my Núll makes a fortune for those thieves.'

He was gasping for breath and Sigurdís was concerned that they might have to take him to hospital. She sat down next to him to try and keep the conversation calm and easy.

'Did you know that he was the real buyer – the one who bought Núll from you?'

'It came as no surprise that that fool Daði was a straw man. I ran into him once and tried to talk to him, but he just scuttled off like a cockroach.'

'So when did you find about Óttar's involvement – in the papers these last couple of days?'

'No. Listen, I'm no idiot. There was a journalist who came here, started asking me about all this. When I'd told him the whole story, he mentioned Daði by name and he asked if I thought he might be a pawn – a front for someone else, as there were rumours going around to that effect. I told him that I hadn't heard anything like that. And I pushed him to tell me what he knew about these rumours. He wouldn't say. But then he asked if I had brought in a consultant to work with me on the company's situation just before we'd had to sell it. And that's when it hit me. That journalist couldn't get away fast enough when I tried to get more out of him...'

His breathing seemed to be made heavier by this long speech, and Sigurdís could see sweat breaking out on his forehead.

'I trusted that wretched man.' These last words came out in a rush and he punched the wall as he spoke.

Sigurdís caught Unnar's eye. She wasn't sure if Guðmundur was in any state to give them a clear answer as to when exactly he had spoken to the journalist. She also wasn't sure that the journalist had indicated Óttar's involvement directly. It was more Guðmundur putting two and two together.

'What happened to your hand?' Sigurdís asked. 'It looks bad. Maybe you ought to get that looked at.'

'That's no fucking business of yours. Now piss off out of here. I've nothing more to say.'

Guðmundur's face was bright red and now sweat was starting to trickle down his cheeks. They decided to leave it at that and thanked him for his time, leaving him sitting on the steps, watching them as they walked away.

'Ugh. He stinks like a brewery, poor old chap,' Unnar said when they were back in the car.

'And more than that – I don't suppose he has a place to wash properly in there. I thought he was going to have a heart attack, poor guy. He's in no physical condition to kill anyone, let alone a fit, healthy man like Óttar.'

'Yeah, you're probably right,' Unnar said, and started the engine.

✳ 28 ✳

Sigurdís had just finished her report on their conversation with Guðmundur Kaldal when Garðar called the team together.

'You've all done a fine job today and reached most of those on the list.'

'We still haven't gotten in touch with some of the foreign individuals who had shares in these two investment companies,' Viktor said. 'We started with the Icelandic investors.'

'That's fine, Viktor. Now, give your impressions of the conversations you've had so far.'

'Unnar and I met Guðmundur Kaldal,' Sigurdís said. 'He's clearly lost everything. He's furious with Óttar and said that he realised for himself there was a link between him and Daði before all this appeared in the media. In that respect we should find out what his movements were around the time Óttar was murdered—'

'But,' Unnar broke in, 'it was our impression after meeting him that he's in no condition to kill anyone, let alone a younger man in excellent health. He could hardly get two sentences out without gasping for breath.'

They gave an account of the man's condition and that there was little chance that he would have been able to make the journey out to Stokkseyri without assistance.

'What about his wife or children? He has sons who are in their twenties, I believe. Couldn't they have assisted?' Garðar asked, his tone sharp. 'Aren't you writing him off too early, after just one visit? You're not healthcare professionals.'

'He and his wife are divorced,' Unnar said shortly. 'I don't know about his boys. If it does turn out to be a revenge killing, are we saying it could have been committed by a whole family? There's been no indication we should consider something like that.' He sounded distinctly irritated.

'We don't rule anything out, and you'll have to check out the sons. This investigation is dragging on and it reflects badly on us if we don't conclude it quickly and effectively. So we have to turn every stone. The media are phoning constantly. When they start running stories about an investigation that's going nowhere – and they will, believe me – that's when my bosses start to get jumpy. Send me your reports when you've spoken to everyone on the list. And I mean *everyone*. Now, get on with it.' And with that Garðar stalked out of the room.

The moment he'd left, they all exhaled sharply, as if they had been holding their collective breath during his final words. They all sat in silence for a moment. Sigurdís had never seen Unnar so truculent. He was the always-cheerful type, using humour to make the best of every difficult situation. But that Unnar had been absent from the meeting and Sigurdís had a wry suspicion that she was seeing a new aspect of his character.

She went over to his desk and suggested that they do as Garðar had suggested, interviewing the other family members before sending their report to Garðar. But Unnar surprised her once more.

'I'm having the same doubts as you, Sigurdís,' he muttered as they made their way out of the station. 'I'm really not sure all this is to do with Óttar's business dealings. The odds that someone found out he was behind all these purchases are so small, I'm inclined to think we should be looking just as carefully into his personal life. If he was able to keep his business activities so secret, who's to say he didn't keep aspects of his private life equally well concealed? The reason he was killed could be something even worse than anything we've found out so far.'

'Yep, I agree. But like you told me, this is Garðar's investigation and seeing how worked up he was earlier, he won't be overjoyed if we go off in some other direction. He'll give us a hell of a bollocking for wasting time on something that he feels is nothing to do with the case.'

'As always, the wise Sigurdís hits the nail on the head. So, we'd best get busy and finish this off so we can show the others what smart detectives we are.'

Sigurdís laughed, pleased to see the cheerful, more familiar Unnar returning.

Sigurdís had a hard time sleeping. This case was going to turn her grey before her time. After speaking to everyone on Elín's list – and their families – they hadn't made any real progress. Guðmundur's wife and sons had little to say about him that was positive, and appeared to have cut him out of their lives. So there was little likelihood that they could have banded together to help him commit murder. The father-and-daughter former owners of Stólar & Borð had a confirmed alibi that placed them in the north of the country at the time the murder had been committed, and the shareholders in the investment businesses seemed to have been prosperous enough in the meantime that they were hardly likely to have wanted to settle scores with Óttar in this manner.

This train of thought about Óttar somehow led her unerringly to the man referred to as her father. But when her mind took her down that road she could be sure there would be no lullabies to rock her to sleep.

Eventually she did manage to doze off and had an uncomfortably vivid dream. She and Unnar walked through the door of her home. As the door closed behind them, he took her in his arms and kissed her passionately. She responded fervently. They said nothing, but went straight into the bedroom and made frenzied love.

Sigurdís was jolted awake, and felt a rush of excitement as she recalled the dream. It had been so real that she could still feel his hands on her body. She'd have to shake this off before going to work. Poor Unnar, wandering unexpectedly into her dreams.

❋

She realised that she must look as if she had come straight from an outdoor festival when she arrived at work. Heading for the meeting room, she ran into Unnar in the corridor.

'I have to say, my dear Sigurdís, that I've rarely seen you looking as radiant as you do on this lovely August morning,' he said, looking her up and down.

Sigurdís pretended to be offended as she answered him back. 'Well thank you, Mr Cocksure. I made every possible effort this morning to meet your demanding standards on personal appearance.'

Then the dream returned to her thoughts and she felt a flush of shame. Was Unnar becoming something more to her than a colleague? He had been good to her and they had become friends, and she was growing to treasure that friendship. And that was the way she wanted to keep it, so although last night's dream was still fresh in her mind and on her body, she decided to shake it off.

They went into the incident room, although with the tension that hung in the air, it would have been better to refer to it as the war room. Garðar looked as if he had spent the last five days at the same outdoor festival she had – he was unshaven, tousled and red-eyed.

'I've been through your reports and I very much appreciate your painstaking work,' he said, without preamble. 'We seem to have taken this investigation down a dead end and I have to admit the possibility that I've concentrated too heavily on the financial angle. Today we need to reboot the investigation and I'm asking you all to cast the net wider. I can hardly believe I'm saying this, but you have a few hours to take a free-style approach to all this.'

Sigurdís glanced enthusiastically in Unnar's direction, and he winked.

'Let's use the time well,' he whispered in her ear.

Back at their desks, they started by drafting a diagram of Óttar's connections around, including all of the main players they knew of, as well as family members, then they worked on developing some scenarios from those. And Sigurdís was ready with her thoughts about Carla and Stephen.

But even though she was pleased to have been given the freedom to explore new angles on the case, Sigurdís struggled to concentrate. Her father and his whereabouts were lingering in her head, so after an hour, she found an excuse to go to Garðar's office.

'Sorry, Garðar. I know you're under pressure, but is there anything new about the old man's efforts to get home from Denmark?'

Garðar gave her a grim smile. 'It doesn't matter how much there is going on here, Sigurdís,' he said. 'You can be certain that I'm keeping tabs on him and I'll let you know the moment something happens. So far, it seems that he still hasn't been able to obtain a ticket for a flight, so let's hope that he's decided to think again.'

'OK.' Sigurdís raised and then dropped her shoulders. 'I can breathe more easily, for the moment.'

She made to leave, but then turned back, her hand still on the door handle.

'There's another thing, while I'm here. I wanted to let you know that the last few days, when you've allowed me to work on this case, have made me really interested in learning more about the investigative side of police work. I haven't checked out what kind of training courses are on offer, or how best to go about learning more, but I'd be grateful to get some advice from you when things are quiet. Would that be OK?'

Garðar gazed at her with tired eyes. 'Is it ever quiet here? But of course I'd be happy to do that for you, and I welcome your interest. You'll do well. You have a critical mind, you're bright and your heart's in the right place.' He stood up, his hand reaching for his cigarettes. 'But right now I'd appreciate it if you go back to the meeting room and make the most of those skills to scope out some new aspects to this investigation. We could certainly do with some.'

He picked up some papers with one hand, an unlit cigarette in the other, and began to look at the pages. But she could see he was staring right through them. She knew when people wanted to be left alone and moreover, she understood why.

When Sigurdís returned to the incident room, Unnar and Viktor had finalised the large diagram of Óttar's connections She stared at it and thought over their current position. They had recovered a significant amount of evidence over the last few days. The problem was that this evidence all supported a different investigation – the case against Óttar himself, and his financial misdemeanours. That case would probably break all records in Iceland as overnight he had become the most controversial figure in the country, albeit posthumously. So they needed to turn away from all that, and focus on other aspects. She had the Carla and Stephen angle, but she needed something closer to home too. She made a decision. They needed to speak to Erla, Óttar's partner, again. Erla had been so devastated when she and Garðar had spoken to her that they hadn't wanted to apply any pressure. So it was quite possible that she had relevant information she'd not mentioned.

Sigurdís picked up the phone and called her.

15.05.1995

He's going to take me away from here. He says I'm his girl, his beautiful girl. I lie and listen as he whispers God's word in my ear. I just shiver with joy. I give myself up to him. Every bit of me is his. We're one before God.

✳ 30 ✳

Erla had asked Sigurdís to come by the legal practice where she worked. She was back at work – it was the best remedy she knew for grief, she said.

Erla's office was just like Erla herself – immaculate and classy. The furniture was elegant and everything was in its place. She was sitting at a large desk, and looked up when Sigurdís came in. They exchanged greetings and Erla invited her to sit on a fashionable blue sofa by the large window that offered a view of Reykjavík harbour.

'I find it soothing to sit here and look out over the harbour, watching the ships come and go. I grew up in the east – in Höfn, on Hornafjörður – and it reminds me of being there. I often open the window just so I can smell the sea.'

She took a seat in a chair facing the sofa. She looked tired and defeated, as if she hadn't been able to rest properly for a long time. Her large, beautiful eyes were puffy and there were clear black shadows under them.

They sat in silence for a while, watching the harbour below, before Sigurdís took the initiative, breaking the ice by asking what Erla had known about the extent of Óttar's business interests.

Erla raised her hands, palms out. 'All this took me completely by surprise. I feel like an idiot. I specialise in contract law, and deal with all kinds of business all day long, and failed to see what was right under my nose. I thought I had been in a relationship with a man who was irreproachable and ambitious, who had everything together. He was widely respected, so I didn't ask any questions. What a fool I was.'

She shook her head with a deep sigh, and looked out at the sea, which was choppy today, beyond the harbour.

'Now I really don't know which way to turn,' she went on, turning back to Sigurdís. 'I turn up here like a robot and apart from that I keep to myself. The wonderful private world I shared with Óttar turned out to be a lie. A complete lie.'

'Were you aware of his friendship with Daði?'

Erla hunched forward, burying her face in her hands. 'I knew nothing. Nothing at all. How's this possible? How did I end up in this mess? I feel as if I've been abducted by aliens and dropped off on the wrong planet. It's all so crazy.'

Sigurdís gave Erla a moment to pull herself together. After a minute or so she sat up straighter, and tucked her hair behind her ears, apparently more in control.

'You mentioned that you had contacted his old friends when you organised the birthday party,' Sigurdís said. 'Could you tell me more about that?'

Erla got to her feet and gazed towards the small boat quay next to the Harpa conference centre, where sails were being hoisted on a smart yacht.

'There's very little that I haven't already told you,' she said in a low voice, still staring out the window. 'I simply found no friends. When I think back on it now, it seems to me that he walked away from each stage of his life and started again in a new place, leaving everything and everyone behind – everyone apart from his mother and sister. I am seeing this all in a new light now, I suppose. Before I was so blinded by love, and his chivalrous façade, that I couldn't see the real him.'

'What about the people he surrounded himself with in recent years?'

'We were always out together, and were constantly being invited here and there. He seemed to know a lot of people, and everyone wanted to know him too, but with hindsight, there was no depth to any of it. The only people he was in touch with on a regular basis were his mother Thrúður and his sister Stefanía. And I even felt that he kept them a little at arm's length. Thrúður called every evening and he would leave some time to speak to her. He never missed a day, but they weren't long conversations. To begin with I interpreted this as a lovely relationship between mother and son, but the more I saw of it, the more it seemed to me that their relationship was cold and a bit robotic, despite the frequent contact.'

She went over to the desk and took a seat on the edge, her hands tucked beneath her thighs.

'Stefanía is absolutely lovely, but even she was like a robot around him. She did everything exactly the same as her mother. I often tried to build a closer relationship with her, something with some depth, but she always backed away.' Sigurdís noticed there were tears in Erla's eyes now. 'I'm sorry. I'm going on about things that don't matter.'

Sigurdís decided to change tack before Erla could get bogged down in sorrow and bring the conversation to an end.

'What do you know about the time he spent in the States?' she asked, watching Erla carefully.

Erla shook her head, turning her lips down. 'I know he went to university there. But not much more. It was years ago, of course. And, as I said, I now have the feeling that he was simply very good at moving on. He didn't mention anything about what he got up to out there, really.'

Sigurdís paused for a moment as she considered what to ask next. Letting Erla come out with new information voluntarily didn't seem to be getting her anywhere. It seemed that the more direct approach was called for.

'Were you aware that he had a son while he was in the US? He's grown up now, of course.'

Erla looked up with startled eyes, and then stared at Sigurdís in growing anguish.

'Now I feel sick. I can't do any more of this.'

She slipped from her perch on the desk, down onto the floor as if she had lost all the strength in her muscles. While Sigurdís knew that the revelations about Ottar's many different lives must come as a shock, she hadn't expected such a physical response.

'Are you all right?' she asked, getting up and approaching Erla.

But Erla made no reply. She drew her knees up to her chin, wrapped her arms around them and stared into space.

There was no way Sigurdís was going to get anything more from Erla this time. She was in no fit state.

'Do you mind, Erla, if we talk again later?' Sigurdís asked.

Again, Erla said nothing. Sigurdís looked around the office and noticed a picture of a smiling young girl.

'Is that your cousin you told us about, the one who lost her life?'

This time Erla looked up.

'Yes. She's always with me. I tried to save her but failed, so every day since I've tried to make up for that.'

She struggled to her feet now, her physique frail and hunched. It seemed to Sigurdís that she had become thinner in the last few weeks.

'You know,' Erla murmured, in such a low voice Sigurdís could barely hear what she was saying. It was as if Erla was disappearing right in front of her. 'I was in a long-term relationship with a man I knew nothing about. I had absolutely no idea who he was.'

31

Óttar Karlsson's funeral took place in Hallgrímskirkja, the largest church in Iceland, towering over the centre of Reykjavik and visible from most places in the city. Sigurdís and Unnar walked up to the graceful church a quarter of an hour before the service was scheduled. A gleaming hearse stood outside as tourists milled about, feverishly snapping pictures of the landmark. Some of them went to the church doors, wanting to explore the grand building, but were turned back when they saw the sign stating that a funeral was due to be held there, and the building would not be open to the public until later in the day.

Sigurdís and Unnar entered through the heavy doors and were met by the undertaker, who handed each of them an order of service. There was a picture of Óttar on the cover, handsome with a faint smile, his assertive presence palpable even from the paper. Sigurdís felt a wave of sadness. Not because of what had befallen Óttar, but more for what he had turned out to be, and for what he had done to people who had loved, trusted and respected him. He had failed them all.

They went through the inner doors and both of them gasped. Although in the wake of the revelations, Óttar had become one of Iceland's most reviled people, they hadn't expected to see a practically empty church for his funeral, a fact made even more brutal by the building's exceptional size. They walked slowly down the aisle and decided to take a seat near the back, where they could watch the service and keep an eye on any mourners.

That wouldn't be difficult. They counted around twenty individuals who had come to see Óttar off, including Thrúður and Stefanía. Erla sat in the next pew, and beside her sat three women of about the same age. Unnar muttered to Sigurdís that it looked as if her friends had come to give her support. Daði sat in the third pew, with a young woman they had not seen before at his side. Unnar pointed out three young ministry officials he recognised sitting with Helgi, the permanent secretary, in the fourth pew.

'The man who was determined to pull all the strings and did everything to build connections and get rich gets a send-off in an almost-deserted church,' Unnar whispered to her. 'There's a lesson to be learned: life's not a game to be played.'

Sigurdís glanced at him and nodded.

The service was tasteful. The priest attempted to tell the story of Óttar's life, he was thin on detail for the last few years, so the emphasis was on his university years and the relationship with his mother and sister.

'A tactful eulogy,' she whispered to Unnar. 'It can't have been easy to prepare.'

He nodded in reply, and pointed out that there were more choristers than there were mourners on the pews.

Bringing the service to an end, the priest thanked everyone for attending, on Thrúður's behalf. The absence of an invitation to a wake was noticeable.

After the ceremony, the casket was not carried out with the mourners following behind, but was left in the church to be taken away by the undertakers later on. However Thrúður and Stefanía did stand by the door, both putting on brave faces, and shook hands with everyone who had attended, thanking them for coming to pay their respects.

Some of the mourners were lingering outside of the church, and Sigurdís and Unnar decided to take the opportunity to speak to them. Sigurdís had only managed to exchange glances with Erla before she jumped into a taxi with her friends immediately after the service was over.

Helgi seemed to be genuinely mourning the loss of a friend. After some chit-chat about the service he told them it was difficult for him to feel any anger towards a dead man. If he had been alive, he would certainly have spoken to him seriously, but under the circumstances there was nothing for it but to be here to say goodbye.

'Some of the guys at work wanted to pay their respects, and I felt it was wrong for them to come without me being here as well. Óttar has left us all hurt, and most of our colleagues don't even want to hear his name mentioned,' he said. 'We're going through his work – all the cases he was dealing with. There aren't many that aren't clear-cut as far as I can see. He appears to have done his work for us well and conscientiously. But considering what has come to light, we can't be certain of anything, so we'll go through everything in fine detail. It's clear now how two-faced he was. So we probably never stood a chance against him, right from the moment he arrived for his interview, with all that media wind in his sails.'

* 32 *

'Shall I make us some coffee, Mum?' Stefanía called from the kitchen of the terraced house on Ásgarður. Thrúður made no reply. 'Even though not many people showed up, the service was beautiful. That was down to you, Mum. You and the priest.'

Stefanía went into the living room and found her mother standing with her arms limp at her sides, staring out through the window.

'I thought I'd been able to make a good man of him, Stefanía.'

'You did your best, Mum. He achieved a lot.'

'If your father hadn't gone, then...'

'Mum, Óttar's behaviour had nothing at all to do with our father. There was always something wrong with him, and if you're finally ready to face it, then so am I.'

Thrúður drew up a chair, with small, slow movements. Just as gradually, she sat down, still looking out of the window.

'This good weather looks like it will be staying with us,' she said at last. 'That'll keep the midges happy.'

Stefanía sighed. 'We don't have to talk about it, Mum. But you know that you did your best. You taught him to take pains over whatever he did, and to keep what you called the dark side of his soul in check.'

'You father had his dark side as well.'

Stefanía went over to her mother, placed her hands on her shoulders and squeezed gently.

'Mum, this is all over now. How about you make us some

pancakes with sugar? Something sweet always makes us feel better.'

'That's a fine idea,' Thrúður said.

She stood up with a little more energy, and made for the kitchen. Stefanía was pleased she'd put her mother back into gear. She had something to do now. Make pancakes with sugar.

Óttar, Óttar, Óttar. He had been her mother's main task in life.

My brother was so good-looking, but he used people, she thought. *He loved to see how far people would go for him. Mum thought she was helping him to keep that dark side in check, but in reality she was just teaching him to hide it all by coming across well. He learned to become accomplished at being immoral. And she was his personal trainer.*

A few minutes later Thrúður brought a small pile of pancakes to the table, and they sat down and ate them silently.

'Perfect pancakes, Mum, as always,' said Stefanía. 'Dead sweet.'

✳ 33 ✳

Garðar burst into the incident room, his hair ruffled and his eyes almost wild.

The whole team turned to him in alarm.

'We have a man in custody who admitted in front of a group of people that he murdered Óttar,' Garðar said with apparent excitement.

There was a murmur round the room as they all took this news in.

'We haven't been able to question him,' Garðar went on, smoothing down his hair and resuming his normal professional demeanour. 'He's sleeping off a drinking session in a cell here.'

He gestured for everyone to gather round so he could brief them on the new developments.

'Staff at a pub called Catalina in Kópavogur called the police last night to come and deal with a difficult customer who was making trouble, throwing chairs around the bar and yelling at people,' he began. 'Three squad cars were sent to fetch him. When he was finally in the back of a car, the staff at the restaurant said that he had already been drunk when he arrived earlier in the evening and said that he was celebrating the death of Óttar Karlsson. But then, later in the evening, he went on a rampage, shouting out that he had murdered him.'

The whole room was silent. Everyone was speechless for a moment. Unnar was first to speak, asking when they would be able to start interrogating the man.

'He's out cold right now, so it's best that we don't waste time, and go to the pub in Kópavogur, talk to the staff, get the names of everyone who was there yesterday and make a start interviewing witnesses. That'll give us some ammunition for when he's in a fit state to talk.'

'Who is he?' Sigurdís asked.

'Well, Sigurdís, it was someone you and Unnar interviewed: Guðmundur Kaldal. It looks like you both underestimated his state of health. He turned out to be strong enough to wreck the place. It's going to need some serious repairs after he went berserk in there last night. The two of you can come with me to Kópavogur so you can see for yourselves what he's actually capable of.'

'Was he gloating?' Unnar whispered to Sigurdís as they followed Garðar out of the room.

'Yes. He couldn't help himself.'

❋ 34 ❋

Unnar dropped heavily into the seat next to Sigurdís.

'You really did the business checking us in. These are the best seats in the plane.'

'It's not rocket science. You just go online as soon as check-in opens, and the seats by the emergency exit are right there waiting.'

'You're clearly way more cosmopolitan than I am. I had no idea you could check in for a flight on the internet,' Unnar said, putting on his seat belt.

The reason Sigurdís knew the quirks of online checking in were because she had spent time studying this over the years, in case she was ever in a position where she couldn't get out of flying somewhere. Unnar had no idea about her fear of flying – or that she had been dreading this trip for the last three weeks, ever since Garðar had announced that they would have to attend this Interpol conference in Brussels on his behalf.

After Guðmundur's surprise confession, Garðar had asked them to attend on his behalf since he needed to stay in Iceland, in case the prosecutor's office needed anything regarding the case. 'It'll be very useful for your job prospects,' he said. 'That's partly why I'm sending Unnar. It's good for his career too.'

She didn't have the heart to tell him about her fear of flying, so until the last moment she hoped he would need them to finish up some details on the case, and they would have to call off their trip. However, the last thing he'd said to her the previous night was, 'Enjoy your time in Brussels.' She just smiled at him, frozen.

As a young girl she had always curled up in a foetal position during take-off. Her routine had always been the same: a silent prayer as the plane roared down the runway, then huddling in her seat. And once the seat-belt signs were switched off, she would head for the toilet to cry.

The visit to the toilet had been added to her routine after one particularly turbulent flight during which she had sat next to Halla, curled up with her face between her knees. She had heard the air hostess ask Halla if the poor girl was feeling all right, if she would like a blanket or some water, and whether she would be able to eat anything? They had continued to talk about her as if she wasn't even there. After that, Sigurdís decided that she would need to keep her cool in future, and developed the routine that helped her hide this debilitating response to any flight she was on. Although it didn't make her fear any less, it gave her the feeling that she had some control of herself and the situation. She had read somewhere that coping mechanisms such as these only prolonged the fear, and did nothing to help her conquer it. But she felt she had no other option.

She was relieved to see that Unnar shut his eyes before the aircraft had even manoeuvred out onto the runway, allowing her to do what she needed to without him noticing. She crossed herself as the plane lifted into the air. She put on her headphones, selected Dikta's 'Thank You', and cranked the volume as high as it would go, clenched her fists and muttered a prayer under her breath: 'Dear God, I'm asking you with all my heart to keep us safe on this flight all the way to Brussels.'

She was pressed back into her seat as the aircraft rose into the sky, felt a ball of fire burning in her stomach, a ball that was about to burst, her heart beat fast and she took a deep breath.

She breathed more easily when the seat-belt light went off

and the air hostesses got to their feet to pull the curtain across to separate first class.

Unnar's head slumped over towards her, his mouth open. He was already snoring. Sigurdís took out her phone and snapped a picture of him. It should have made her smile, but her fear of flying meant that she wasn't able to think logically while in the air. Her thoughts were scattered in different directions. She tried to watch a film she had downloaded to her phone, but was unable to concentrate. So she switched on the screen on the back of the seat in front and tracked the flight's progress. They had passed the Faroe Islands and as the map shifted, she saw that they would soon pass Denmark.

Garðar had told her the day before that the old bastard had finally scraped together enough for a flight to Iceland, and it was booked for two weeks from now. She had taken the decision to not tell Halla and Einar until she came home. She didn't know what Garðar intended to do about it, or even if he would be able to do anything. She suspected that he would try to meet Agnar as soon after his arrival as possible and persuade him to leave the country. But Sigurdís knew that this was no real solution. He would always be a threat to all of those connected to him. He would continue to terrify and infuriate them, wherever he might be in the world. At least, for as long as he was alive. Sigurdís surprised herself by hoping that his arteries were furred up, or his liver was swollen from alcohol, or his heart was...

She shuddered, quickly shaking off such thoughts. She didn't want to think this way.

The map on the screen had pulled out for a moment, and now included North America. Her thoughts went to her conversation with Carla and to Stephen's visit to Iceland. She'd felt all the way through the investigation into Óttar's death that his time in America was somehow connected to his death. And this feeling still refused to leave her, even though Guðmundur

Kaldal's case had been referred to the prosecutor and was now in the process of being prepared for his court appearance. Something about his confession just didn't ring true for Sigurdís. But something about Carla set her antennae twitching.

'That was a pleasant flight,' Unnar said cheerfully as they disembarked at Zaventeem Airport in Brussels.

Sigurdís was determined to keep to herself the agonising anxiety she had been through, along with the burning muscles, the headache and the loss of appetite that went with it. She wondered if she could hitch a ride back to Iceland on a merchant ship.

Instead she put on a teasing voice: 'You didn't have to put up with yourself snoring with your mouth open the whole time.'

He laughed. 'I'll make it up to you by being the perfect travelling companion. We can be tourists for what's left of today. We don't often get the chance to take it easy somewhere abroad, so we should make the most of it.'

Sigurdís was pleased to hear it, and admitted to herself that she was looking forward to spending some of the time in Brussels with Unnar. Her feelings when she was in his presence were different now, and had been ever since her dream of the two of them making love. It had been so vivid that she could still feel the pressure of his hands.

The hotel was a comfortable one near Grand Place. Sigurdís put her small suitcase on the bed as soon as she was in her room and walked over to the narrow window that ran all the way to the floor. She opened it and smiled as the hubbub of the traffic and the bustle on the street hit her. She had a sudden urge to dive in and taste everything this city had to offer. The flight was behind her, forgotten, and now it was time to lose herself in a big city. Her preference was to sit somewhere, have a meal in the sunshine, and watch people go about their days. She had seen from the car on the way to the hotel that people were still sitting outside bars, enjoying the mild autumn weather.

She turned from the window, dropped onto the bed and felt herself floating on a cloud. The room was small, but very clean, and expense hadn't been spared when it came to the mattress and pillows. But the bed could wait until the evening. It was time to unpack and make a move. After the torture of the flight, she deserved to spend time on something other than sleep and work. It was as well to make the most of it, as Unnar had put it. He had told her he would come and find her once he had taken a shower, but she couldn't wait. She wanted to be outside, losing herself in a big, busy city.

The first thing Sigurdís saw when she emerged from the hotel was huge mural of Audrey Hepburn on the building next door. On closer inspection she saw it was an advertisement for an exhibition about the life of this beautiful actress. Deciding to take a look inside, she saw right away that this was something for her, bought a ticket and began to look around. There was so much to see. She discovered that Hepburn's son had been involved in setting up the exhibition and had illustrated a book about his mother's life.

When she'd completed her tour, Sigurdís bought the book in the gift shop, and also a scented candle that was supposed to produce an aroma just like Audrey's.

As she left the exhibition, she walked straight into Unnar.

'Is this as far as you've got?' he asked.

'I took a look in here,' she said, gesturing towards the gallery.

'Audrey Hepburn! One of the most beautiful women ever, in my opinion. Delicate but still tough. A bit like you.' He gave her a quick grin and looked at her from under his eyebrows. 'Was it interesting?' he went on.

Sigurdís flushed slightly and gave him a quick description of what she had seen. Unnar listened with interest, and then mentioned food. He was starving, and suggested Hotel Metropole, one of the most famous buildings in the city and a flagship of the Art Deco movement there.

'I had no idea you were a man of culture,' Sigurdís said with a smile.

Unnar replied that he made an effort to take people by surprise.

'But to be serious for a moment,' he continued, 'when I was younger I really wanted to study architecture and spent a lot of time learning about different architectural periods. I suppose I was a nerd, really. But then as I grew up public service began calling more strongly than architecture. I saw a programme on the telly about police work, and decided I wanted to apply.'

'That was a real about-face,' she said, finding the change of track a little odd.

'I told you,' Unnar smiled, 'I'm full of surprises.'

Hotel Metropole stood out from the rest of the street, like an old-time film star dressed up in the fashion of the time and clinging on to a century-old image. They took a table at Café Metropole on the ground floor, and the waiter handed them menus, addressing them in French. Unnar dropped yet another surprise by replying to the man in the same language.

'You really are a man of mystery,' Sigurdís said. 'Where did you learn to speak French?'

A distant look appeared on Unnar's face for a moment, and he told her about a year spent as an exchange student while he had been at high school.

'As I said, I was going to be an architect, and that means you have to get to know Paris, y'see. I was there for a year. It was a fantastic time. I picked up French quite quickly, and I've taken care to keep using it by reading quite a lot in French. Mostly books and French websites. The gossip magazines are a great way to keep language skills alive!'

'And what's the news in the world of French celebrity?'

'You don't want to know, Sigurdís. You don't want to know.'

When they had ordered, Sigurdís surveyed the restaurant around her. The place was certainly showing its age. The original Art Deco stylings were still present, as Unnar pointed out to her. But he also pointed to places where later fashions had been added here and there.

Sigurdís found that the ketchup bottles on every table clashed with it all, though, and it occurred to her that if she were to write a review of the place, the title would read 'Art Deco with a Side Order of Ketchup'.

✳ 35 ✳

Sigurdís awoke, rested after a deep, sound sleep. She and Unnar had spent a great day together, which came to an end with a nightcap at the hotel bar. In the lift, going up to her room, she'd felt a touch of regret that the evening was over. That wasn't what she wanted, which was a new feeling for her when she was in a man's company. She smiled inwardly as she thought of Unnar.

'Time to get a grip on yourself, woman,' she said to herself out loud. 'He is your friend, and that's all. Just take what you can and run with it.'

She had already fallen in love with Brussels, and toyed with the idea of more travel around the world. Maybe she ought to try out that fear-of-flying course Dóra had mentioned. She wouldn't be going far otherwise. But right now she was determined to make the most of the moment, so she quickly got herself ready to go downstairs and meet Unnar for breakfast.

He had already started by the time she made an appearance.

'I must warn you, Sigurdís, it's proper hippy food here. Everything's organic, and it's mostly vegetables and seeds. Pretty good, all the same.'

Sigurdís couldn't conceal her disappointment that she wouldn't have bacon and eggs, cooked by someone else, most importantly. She chose Greek yoghurt and smothered it with fruit and seeds.

'Well, we get fresh fruit that someone has cut up for you, that's something,' she said to Unnar as she took a seat.

He looked good for a night's sleep, dressed in his conference suit, his hair slightly damp.

'Garðar called me last night,' he said through a mouthful of seeds. 'The prosecutor isn't certain the case against Guðmundur is strong enough to secure a conviction. Garðar has to go through the whole case again with Viktor to put together answers to the prosecutor's questions.'

Sigurdís wasn't surprised. The only piece of real evidence was what he had blurted out, drunk and in a bar. Guðmundur had told the bar staff and other customers that he was celebrating Óttar Karlsson's death – and that part seemed the truth. But later in the evening he had become seriously intoxicated, raucously raising glass after glass to Óttar's death. It had been when the bar staff had asked him to stop, offering to call him a cab, that his temper had snapped and he had run rampage through the place, hurling chairs and anything in his way aside, yelling that he could kill them all, just like Óttar. He swore he'd leave them all lying on the beach, just like that scoundrel Óttar. Several witnesses were in agreement that his words could only be understood as a confession of murder.

Sigurdís agreed that his words could be interpreted in that way, but thought there were other ways to read them too. It also had to be taken into account that Guðmundur's mind was addled by years of drinking. That night he had been so drunk that it had been almost twenty-four hours before he had been fit to be questioned. He had no recollection of the previous evening and admitted that events over the last few years had become foggy in his mind. He had been in a bad way during the interview, appearing confused and unable to account for his movements on the evening of Óttar's murder. He admitted his hatred for the man, but said that he didn't believe he had murdered him. The unfortunate man couldn't be certain, however, as there were long periods that had slipped from his memory. Once a lawyer had been appointed for him, he refused to say anything more, other than that he intended to plead not guilty.

The burden of proof became heavier when it was found there was little or no physical evidence connecting him to Óttar. There was nothing found on the body or at Guðmundur's room at the old industrial unit to indicate that he had any recent contact with Óttar, or even that he had met him over the past few years.

'I'm not convinced he did this,' Sigurdís said, after her musings.

'And you know that I agreed with you, Sigurdís. I do think it's farfetched, but taking everything into consideration – not least his confession at the bar – you have to admit that most likely we were wrong. Even their phones were traced as being in the same area at the time of the murder.'

Sigurdís sighed. 'I know all that, but we didn't look closely at where Guðmundur went that evening and how he travelled out east. The area they were both traced to is a large one, so there's no certainty that they were anywhere near each other, really. It's not strong enough evidence, so I can understand why the prosecutor has doubts, especially as Guðmundur now denies having murdered Óttar.'

Unnar gazed back at her, looking as if he was uncertain whether to agree with her, or to stick with the case Garðar and the team had put together.

'In any case, I'm supposed to be working on this with Garðar and Viktor when we get back tomorrow,' Unnar said as he got to his feet. 'And we don't have anything other than Guðmundur to hand. Elín hasn't found any evidence of any wrongdoing on Óttar's part during his time in the ministry. So Garðar doesn't think there's anything to be gained by investigating his colleagues further, and practically every other lead we had has been ruled out by now.'

She stood up too, and a silence fell between them, as if they'd agreed not to discuss this issue any further.

Sigurdís couldn't help herself though, and as they made their way to the lift, she said, 'Not every lead has been ruled out. We didn't talk to Carla or Stephen again.'

Unnar didn't respond.

'It wouldn't hurt to reach out to her again,' she began, but Unnar stopped her.

'We are not doing anything without Garðar's involvement or approval. So get this out of your head while we are still working on Guðmundur's case. Can you imagine if it were to get out that Garðar's own people didn't believe in the case they'd help put together? That would have a huge effect on the department, and especially on Garðar. I know you don't want that, and I certainly don't.'

This lecture took Sigurdís a little aback. She understood what Unnar was saying, but at the same time she knew she just had to call Carla again. She would do it from the hotel that afternoon, when they had returned from the conference. She had to find out more about Óttar and his time in America. It couldn't hurt to try getting some more background on him, and neither Unnar nor Garðar would have to know.

36

'Hi Carla, this is Sigurdís Hölludóttir from the Icelandic Police,' Sigurdís said, trying to make her voice bright, but professional. 'Do you remember me? I called you before, about the death of Óttar Karlsson?'

Carla hesitated, and greeted her weakly. 'Yes, I remember our conversation.'

'Do you have a few minutes for me now, I would like to ask you a few more questions?'

There was a long silence, and Sigurdís could sense her reluctance.

'Yes. I guess so. But I don't have much time.'

Sigurdís started by asking how Carla and Óttar had met.

'I understand it was through a religious movement. Is that correct?'

Carla said that her information was indeed correct; at that time she had been part of a small religious group in Minnesota. The leader of the group, a man who called himself John Smith, would often disappear from the old farmhouse where they all lived for a few days at a time. On one such occasion, he returned with a young man by his side: Óttar. The two of them had met at a casino on a reservation a few hundred miles away.

Those living in the farmhouse with John Smith were mostly young women who had, for various reasons, found themselves in dire straits. He had helped them out of their difficult circumstances and provided them with shelter, wanting, he said, to give them a good start in life and provide them with the security that none of them had been able to find at home. And in this way, after a while, he had formed something of a band of followers.

John had clearly been impressed by Óttar, and, importantly, he trusted him around the girls.

Carla's voice was robotic and Sigurdís suspected that she was getting the edited version of the story. Carla ended the tale by explaining that she had become pregnant, and shortly after that, Óttar had vanished. She hadn't seen him again and knew no more about him or what he had done with his life.

Sigurdís was intrigued by the story, and was ready to ask more questions – about the community, and especially about the nature of Carla's relationship with Óttar, but Carla said a quick goodbye and hung up before she could continue.

Sigurdís sat on the hotel bed in disappointment with how abruptly Carla had ended the call.

'What aren't you telling me, Carla?' she muttered to herself.

Once again, she had a deep longing to meet her in person, speak to her face to face. But that could be a challenge, as the Atlantic Ocean and more lay between them. And there was the little issue of Garðar, and his view on the direction the investigation should take. On top of that, her only ally, Unnar, had also dismissed the idea.

She walked to the window and glanced at her phone. Then stared out at the street for a moment, and idea forming in her mind.

Finally, she shook herself. She'd made a decision. She tapped a message to Dóra into her phone:

Hæ, Dóra. I'm going with you to NY at the weekend! I'll get a direct flight from Brussels and meet you there.

A reply from Dóra wasn't long in coming.

YESSSS! Followed by a string of emojis.

Sigurdís didn't mention that her trip would start in

Minnesota before heading for New York. She took a deep
breath, then called Garðar and asked if it was OK to take a
week's holiday at the last minute, to spend some time travelling
with friends.

He seemed relieved to hear of her travel plans, telling her to
enjoy the trip and leave all the stress behind. They would see each
other in a week.

37

It was probably the craziest thing she had ever done, going online to book a flight from Brussels to Minnesota and boarding the plane the very next morning. She had spoken to Dóra the night before and given her an outline of what she had in mind. Although Dóra supported her completely, she seemed concerned.

'I know you're finally getting out of your comfort zone, and I applaud that, but does it really have to be in such a big way? How about starting with smaller steps?' she asked, then forced a laugh and said that if Sigurdís wasn't in New York on Saturday, she would report her missing.

After promising to call every day until they were due to meet in four days' time, Sigurdís made Dóra agree not to mention what she was doing to anyone.

'Bye, scatterbrain,' Dóra said at the end of the call.

Sigurdís felt bad lying to Garðar, and even worse when she had stood in the doorway of Unnar's hotel room last night, lying to his face. It had been an awkward moment. He had invited her in, but she had faked a headache. She knew he would see right through her if she spent more than five minutes with him.

Sigurdís was sat in row thirty of a KLM airliner flying to Atlanta, from where she would pick up a connection to Minnesota. There hadn't been time to go through her usual anxiety routine, and she was surprised to find that she felt OK without it. She was in a middle seat in a middle row, which was something she would certainly not have chosen, but somehow it didn't matter. More than likely she was so excited about what was ahead that her fear of flying had been elbowed aside.

In truth, she had no idea what was waiting for her – whether or not Carla would agree to speak to her, and if she would be able to meet Stephen, Carla and Óttar's son. Sigurdís tried to imagine what mother and son looked like, and then tried to visualise a young Óttar as a member of a religious group. He seemed so far from the type who would be attracted by a religious congregation. As they'd learned these last few weeks, he was the kind of person who wanted to control everything around him. Maybe that was exactly the point? Perhaps the community had been fertile ground for someone like him, who loved to manipulate others, playing games the rules of which he'd written himself. She was determined to find out what role he had played. The Óttars of this world didn't join religious groups to find themselves – they joined because they wanted something from someone, and she was going to find out what it had been and if it had followed him to the beach by Stokkseyri almost thirty years later.

38

Sigurdís had never been to the States before, but she had landed in Minneapolis, had hired a car and was now trying to find her way through the traffic jams on her way out of the twin cities of Minneapolis and St Paul. Despite the dressing-down she knew awaited her back in Iceland, this felt absolutely the right thing to have done.

She punched the name of the town where Carla lived, Biwabik, into the navigation system. A google search had told her that around a thousand people lived in this place, and that it was one of Minnesota's natural beauty spots. She got the impression it was a popular place for outdoorsy people to visit, and Sigurdís was more excited about visiting it than experiencing the bustle and noise of Manhattan. Maybe one day she would drag Dóra on a road trip that was about more than just bars and pink cocktails. They were so different that she sometimes failed to understand why Dóra bothered with her. High-life Dóra and straight-and-narrow, low-key Sigurdís. They were a strange pair.

Four hours behind the wheel brought her finally to Biwabik. The main street looked as if it had been pulled directly from a movie about small-town America. Few people were about. The houses were low, built of timber or brick, with a couple of stores, and one restaurant. She looked around for a place to relax for a moment. She had driven the whole distance without a break, and now she needed to stretch her legs before knocking on

Carla's door. The unfortunate Carla, who had not woken up this morning expecting a visit from an Icelandic police officer gone rogue. For a moment her confidence of earlier left her, and it occurred to Sigurdís that she was in fact nothing more than a stalker in an Icelandic police uniform, someone who couldn't let go once an idea had taken hold in her head. What on earth was she thinking, travelling all this way to dig into the past of a woman who had made it clear she wanted nothing to do with this investigation?

She parked in front of a shop that had a sign proclaiming that it was a hardware store, but in fact seemed to stock, not just tools, but every possible item – a wigless mannequin in a green dress had been arranged in the window next to an armchair. Sigurdís smiled, finding it quaint. She walked on further, past an ice-cream place where a young man with two small children were picking their flavours, before coming to a small park that could well be a meeting point for the people of Biwabik.

There were plenty of well-cared-for conifers and a bandstand where Sigurdís imagined a brass band playing on special occasions and a mayor in his regalia making a speech for the townspeople. Not far away stood a large statue of an elk. She went over to it, wondering what an elk had done to deserve such a position of honour. She guessed that there were hunting grounds around here, and the affection for the elk was because they had kept people alive through the centuries. She was considering the relationship between elks and people when she heard a man's voice behind her.

'That's Honk – a real elk. He made himself at home here one winter around a hundred years ago and caused some trouble. People had noticed his tracks in the snow and they could hear him calling in the night. Some boys found him in a stable and gave him something to eat. He was no fool, this old guy. After that he became part of the town, until he moved on in the spring. People were pretty fond of him and there have been stories about Honk ever since. Not much happens around here, you see – then or now. So Honk's visit was a dash of excitement – broke up the monotony. A teacher around here wrote a children's book about him a few decades ago. Phil Stong was his name. Won an award for it. Went on to become pretty famous, I understand.'

'Wow. Interesting story,' Sigurdís said, turning to look at him.

'I'm sorry. I didn't introduce myself. Hank Finkelman. I sit on the town council here in Biwabik, and I run the diner along the street.' He gestured behind him.

Sigurdís smiled and introduced herself with the story she'd concocted while on the road. He was a tourist on a road trip who wanted to see a pretty US small town, she picked this one from the map and had known as soon as she had driven into town that she had made the right choice. She carefully made no mention of Carla, cautious not to say anything that would set the local rumour mill going and cause her problems. She knew nothing about Carla or her situation, and in the town as small as this, Hank could easily turn out to be her neighbour. At any rate, there had to be a good chance that they knew each other.

Hank appeared to be delighted at her interest in his town, and told her she was in just the right place if small-town life was what she was looking for.

'Are you from Sweden?' he asked confidently, certain that he had hit the nail on the head.

She replied with a smile that he was close, but not quite, and told him she was from Iceland.

'Then you must know all about small-town life. Plenty of them there, surely? I've always wanted to visit Iceland, right up until that volcano of yours messed things up,' he said, and made a valiant attempt to pronounce Eyjafjallajökull.

Sigurdís couldn't help laughing And decided not to go into

any details about how Eyjafjallajökull was actually a glacier that sat on top of the volcano.

'You know that immigrants from Scandinavia, especially Finland, played a big part in this town's history?' Hank said. 'They came and settled here, and you can see the Scandinavian influence in the style of buildings.'

This was something Sigurdís hadn't been aware of. It was an interesting connection – one she banked for consideration later. She thanked Hank, and they didn't part until he'd extracted a promise from her to call in on him at the diner while she was in town.

Carla lived in a tiny house not far from the main street. It was a neat little box of a house with a steeply pitched roof, and was painted pale yellow with red window frames. It looked well cared for, and the modest garden clearly got all the attention it needed. Sigurdís walked hesitatingly up the steps to the red front door, uncertain of what sort of reception she would get. She knocked cautiously and the door was answered by a tiny woman with jet-black hair, dark eyes and a pale complexion, who looked to be about the same age as Sigurdís. This couldn't be Carla. Sigurdís had been expecting someone considerably older.

'Can I help you?' the small woman asked, and Sigurdís instantly recognised her voice.

'Carla Abraham?'

'Yes,' she replied, with some hesitation. 'Do we know each other?'

As Sigurdís introduced herself Carla's eyes widened and her mouth dropped open in astonishment.

'What brings you all the way here?' she asked, her hand gripping the door frame. 'I told you everything. And ... and I read that you already have someone in custody – he confessed to Óttar's murder.'

Sigurdís noted that Carla must clearly have gone out of her way to follow the case. She doubted a murder in Iceland would have been reported on the US evening news.

She nodded, and said that, yes, they had someone currently

in custody, but that so much had come to light during the investigation, she still needed to know more about Óttar and his past.

'And I was in the neighbourhood anyway. I'm travelling to New York on Saturday to meet some friends and it felt like a good idea to make a trip of it.'

That made Carla laugh, and Sigurdís immediately felt at ease.

'It's not exactly in the neighbourhood, and America is a big place. You must be really committed to your job.' Carla paused and scrutinised Sigurdís's face for a moment, as if trying to decide on something. Then she smiled again and said, 'Look, why don't you come on in. If we're going to chat, better to do it in comfort rather than on the doorstep.' And Sigurdís felt sure she'd won the woman over. Once again, she felt her decision to come here was the right one.

Carla's home turned out to be much like its owner – small, pretty and neat. There were few items of furniture and everything had its place. There was nothing unnecessary and nothing gaudy. It reminded Sigurdís of her own place. She never understood why people needed to fill their homes with junk that had no purpose but to make their lives more complicated. Life was busy enough already without having to dust the rubbish as well.

Carla showed her into a small, warm living room and gestured for her to take a seat on an elegant old sofa. There was little on the walls other than one framed print of flowers, and a few photographs of a young man. This was undoubtedly Stephen, Sigurdís decided, and she was sure she noticed a resemblance to Óttar.

'I'm sorry, but I can't offer you much except water or coffee and a sandwich,' Carla said.

Sigurdís accepted the offer of a glass of water and a sandwich. The bread turned out to be home-made and some of the best she had ever tasted.

'How long have you lived here, Carla?' Sigurdís asked, sipping at the water.

Carla put her coffee cup aside and said that she had moved into the house twenty-two years ago. She had wanted to live somewhere peaceful, where Stephen could grow up in safe surroundings.

'When I was a kid, I read a book about Honk the Elk – whose statue you will have passed on your way here.' Sigurdís nodded and said she'd seen him. 'Well,' said Carla, 'the book's based on real events that took place around here a hundred or so years ago. And I thought that if the people in this place showed such compassion for an elk that wandered into their town one cold winter, then they had to be good people. And I was right. It's a great place to be. Life is simple, and good.'

Sigurdís told Carla that she'd met Hank by the statue, and about how friendly he was, and they talked for a while about the charms of the town and the quality of life that went with being so close to nature. Finally Carla, paused and fixed her gaze on Sigurdís, scrutinising her once again.

'But you haven't come such a long way to chat about life in a small town, have you? And Biwabik certainly isn't on the way from Europe to New York. So it must be really, very important to you to hear what I have to say about Óttar.'

Sigurdís nodded seriously. 'It is. I think what you know about him might be essential to this case. I realise you didn't want to say much—'

Carla interrupted her: 'Look, I've had time to think about all this now. The father of my son is dead, and it seems to me that it's now time ... that it's now time to lay everything on the table. I wasn't sure how to do it, or when. But you've come all this way. So why not you? Why not now?'

Sigurdís bit her tongue, not wanting to say a word in case Carla changed her mind.

194 | KATRÍN JÚLÍUSDÓTTIR

'So, yes, I'll tell you everything and won't leave anything out,' Carla said and then paused for a moment before continuing, looking away from Sigurdís now. 'I've never told Stephen the whole story. He believes that his father was just a young, irresponsible guy who couldn't face the pressures of bringing up a child, and that's why he left. It's time to tell him all this as well. And I will ... I will. But it will help if I tell you first.'

It was close to midnight when they parted. Sigurdís left the house behind her and stood by the car in the darkness. The silence of the night and the tale Carla had told her made her want to lie down in the street beside the car and look up at the stars until life could again be something beautiful. She had listened for hours to Carla's incredible account of how she had ended up as part of the religious group run by John Smith – whose real name had been Peter Adamsson – of her life as part of the congregation, and of the time from when Óttar appeared to when he left, and everything in between.

Sigurdís felt the rage grow inside her. *The poor child*, she thought, because Carla had been no more than a child at the time when she had encountered these men.

She had been just a child when she bore a child of her own – Óttar's child.

✱ 40 ✱

Carla came from a completely ordinary middle-class American family. They'd lived in St Paul, and she'd enjoyed a pleasant childhood with her parents and older sister. But everything had changed when she was eight years old and her father lost his life in a workplace accident. Her mother had been a housewife and found it difficult to find a job, especially work that would enable them to maintain their lifestyle. They moved to a small rented apartment over a shop in the city. Her mother eventually found a laundry job that meant long working days, and the two girls were often left to look after themselves. Carla didn't recall exactly when it happened, but at some point the sisters realised that their mother had been drinking increasingly heavily. It finally led to her losing her job. And that was when their world really came crashing down.

One morning the sisters woke up and started their day, as so often, by clearing away the mess after the drinking session their mother had continued after the nearby bar had closed. This time one of the partygoers had stayed over. Carla remembered how they had screamed when a naked, drowsy man appeared from their mother's bedroom. He responded by telling them to shut the hell up, went to the fridge for a couple of beers, before heading back to the bedroom and closing the door behind him.

He was there to stay. This new man of their mother's was an even heavier drinker than she was, and he expected them to cater to his every whim. To start with, he demanded that the girls keep the place clean, do the shopping and bring anything the two of them wanted, while they just sat and drank.

It was their mother's job to look after his needs in bed. But after a while, he took to demanding that the door stayed open while he had sex with her, and sometimes he would tell them to sit still on the sofa while they had their fun on the dining table. He wanted them to watch. Carla recalled the terror they endured and how they hoped that the table would collapse while they were at it, so they would drop through the floor and disappear. It was a revolting experience and frequently she'd not even been sure her mother was properly conscious.

One day, when Carla was ten and her sister thirteen, a woman from child protection appeared with two police officers. She told them to pack a case, as she had a court order for them to be removed from the household. Carla's sister had told a friend of their mother's that the new guy had started to abuse her, had already been groping her for some time. The friend hadn't hesitated to inform the child-protection authorities. Carla recalled being angry with her sister, because she had always hoped that their mother would sober up, throw the guy out and everything would be fine once again. In spite of all her problems, surely her mother had to love her children more than the bottle.

They were each sent to foster homes. Carla's sister began to dabble in drugs, and eventually they lost contact. For a long time, Carla was shuttled from one foster home to another, but she always lived in hope, waiting for her mother to fetch her, sober and wracked with regret. Carla was so convinced that she must be fighting to get them back that one day she took a bus to the apartment over the shop. But her mother was gone. Carla had no idea where, and never heard from her again.

From then on, life was a battle for Carla. The mirage of hope that had kept her spirits up had vanished, and she gradually became numb and apathetic. She began to fail in some subjects at school and was given detentions. Sometimes she would misbehave deliberately, simply so she would be made to stay in detention, as that was better in her eyes than spending time at the foster home. She also struggled to form relationships with other people, and became increasingly introverted. She wandered the streets, looking for her sister, her mother – hoping to see them, hoping they were hiding from the authorities somewhere and would come to get her.

On one such excursion, when she was eleven, she met a man who called himself John Smith. That day, despairing of her situation, she had broken down in tears on a bench in a corner of a park frequented by homeless people. An unattractive young man, who was clearly in a bad way, had sat down next to her, putting his arms around her and saying he would comfort her. It was as she sat there, stiff with fear, that John Smith appeared like an angel and shooed the young man away. He gave her a can of soda and led her away from the park. She was so grateful to him, when he suggested he take her to a diner, she said yes. They had another soda and then he offered her a meal, and by the end of it she'd told him her whole story.

He was good to her, and attentive. He told her that he owned a beautiful farm outside the city in a peaceful place near a town called Bemidji. His role in life, he told her, was to help those who were lost – people like her. He gave her a phone number, told her she could call whenever she wanted to, and he would come and fetch her. But she wasn't to tell anyone, as the authorities didn't approve of his methods. They were too firmly wedded to their system of foster homes, he said. And she couldn't help but agree with him when he said they only made things worse for the children who stayed in them, failing to provide them with the security they needed. He showed her newspaper cuttings that proclaimed how badly children were treated at the state's foster homes. Carla already knew this from her own experience but she was comforted to have found in John Smith someone who clearly understood this.

'God sent me to find you,' he said.

Not even two weeks had passed before Carla called him, once more in despair about her foster home and her loneliness. He picked her up, just as he said he would, and she went with him to the farm where her life was to begin anew. He called it a new beginning. His words were music to her ears.

The farmhouse was old, but beautiful. At one time the farm had been prosperous. The house itself was stately, with two storeys and a veranda that ran all the way around it. At the back was a small guest house and a toolshed, and two large barns stood not far away. It was in a remote location, surrounded by trees and greenery, and seemed like a paradise to a frightened girl who the city had swallowed up and then spat out. She was exhausted when she arrived, but felt an inner contentment for the first time since her father's death.

There were four young girls living there. One was roughly her own age, two a few years older and the eldest was around eighteen. They all wore simple blue dresses, their hair braided, and they were clean, neat and gentle. They made Carla feel welcome and led her up the stairs to the bedrooms, showing her to a bright, warm room with an old-fashioned bed with a metal frame. In a corner by the window stood a wooden chair, beside which stood a table with a pretty bronze lamp. Opposite the bed was a white chest of drawers on which stood a small glass vase filled with fresh flowers. To Carla's eyes, it was a heavenly, peaceful place. In fact the whole house had a welcoming feel to it, and it was with relief that she placed her bag of belongings on the bed.

Soon Carla found herself enjoying the daily routines in the farmhouse. Each of them had their own defined tasks. It was Carla's job to help the eldest girl to prepare meals and clear away afterwards.

Each day began with John leading prayers. They stood in a circle, holding hands, and he would fall into a trance as he spoke God's words. He claimed they came to him directly from the Creator.

Carla very quickly came to believe that God did indeed speak through John. He was unlike anyone else she had known, and in time she placed all her trust in him. On her twelfth birthday, he took her aside to offer her a direct conversation with God. She was overjoyed, as she knew that John did this with the other girls, and this was her first time. Up to now, he had said that she wasn't ready, that there was still too much of her old, bad life obstructing her. That day she was served her favourite breakfast – oatmeal with cream and blueberries – after which she was given a blue dress, the same as the other girls wore, and was told that she would have no chores that day. The other girls took her in their arms and celebrated. She felt the warmth of real sisterhood – secure, seen and protected.

From that day on, she regularly met John for a conversation direct with God. With hindsight, as an adult, she saw she'd been groomed and subjected to systematic brainwashing. She was supposed to be obedient to God and to John, as he was the Lord's representative on Earth. She was expected to do her chores and to work on her own personal side in private sessions with John. He was the key to her future.

Carla couldn't remember when John had begun to abuse her. At the time she hadn't see it as abuse or anything wrong at all, but simply as a physical interaction with God. She had witnessed her mother's obscene coupling with her boyfriend. But this was different; it seemed to her at the time as beautiful and caring. She even enjoyed these sessions with John. They made her feel secure, special – even unique. So she failed to make the connection and understanding what was really happening to her.

John had a habit of taking short trips away, normally a few

days at a time. On the surface, things at the farm didn't change much when he was away, as the girls would continue to manage the daily running of the place. He made sure they had everything they needed and always allocated tasks to the girls before leaving, and their days would go much as usual. The eldest girl led them through their prayers, which convinced Carla still further of John's connection to the Almighty, as this girl was not able to make the prayer sessions as moving as John did. She was mechanical and cold, with no indication that she was in touch with God. They all missed John during his absences, and often became insecure, worried that all the evil in the world would break its way through to them without John's presence. So there was always a heartfelt welcome for him on his return.

One day, when John returned from one of these trips, he brought with him a young and exceptionally pleasant young man, who he introduced to the girls as Óttar. Óttar Karlsson, from Iceland. They were naturally curious, as John had never before brought a guest back to the farm, so they stood and stared at this new, heavenly man. John said he had encountered him on the Chippewa tribe's reservation. Carla now knew it was most likely that they had met at one of the casinos the tribe ran, but John could of course not tell them that. He was a 'holy' man, in all the inverted commas possible. Spiritual men such as John didn't go to casinos.

Óttar and John got on extremely well, and after a few days John told the girls that he had believed God spoke only through him, that was until he met Óttar. God spoke through him as well, he told them. The girls were delighted, considering themselves fortunate, that they had been chosen to be taken care of by such great men. They squealed and chattered. They watched Óttar and followed him everywhere.

Then he chose her. Over all the other girls. He chose her for his special companion. Little Carla. She was proud and deeply happy. When they were together he was so caring, and exciting too. He was young, handsome and said such lovely things. He called her his sweet and sometimes he would hold her tight as they lay together naked after communing with God, whispering to her that she wasn't just his sweet but was a whole bowl of sugar. He was gentler than John, and she wanted to be with him. Perhaps this was because he was closer to her age, even though there were about twelve years between them. He was a young man and she was a child. But in her lost child's mind she dreamed of a future with him.

She had just turned thirteen when she realised that her body was changing. Her breasts were tender, she was often nauseous and very tired. Two of the other girls were feeling the same as Carla and they were convinced that they all had caught the same flu. The eldest girl decided to speak to John and seek his guidance. He went pale when he heard, which terrified the girls as they assumed that as they had the same symptoms, they must be seriously ill, or at death's door.

From then on the relationship between Óttar and John soured and the atmosphere in the house changed dramatically. Óttar's behaviour during his meetings with Carla altered too. Instead of connecting Carla with God through his body, Óttar took to lecturing her for hours on end. He spoke quietly, his voice captivating, half whispering in her ear that she was special, that she had been chosen. But after a few weeks his tone changed and became darker.

By this time her belly was starting to swell and he told her this was because she was full of sin. He and John had tried to help her, but her sins were so great and so deep-rooted that the Devil kept returning and now he had made a nest for himself inside her. She was terrified, with no notion of what she should do. John was hardly to be seen and seemed to be avoiding her. And the older girls did the same, as if they didn't want to be infected.

One day Óttar called her into his room to speak to him, and told her that there was only one way to expel the Devil from her body, and that was through direct connection with God. He knew how to do this and would help her. She was deeply relieved and so grateful that she threw her arms around him. He told her to wait until evening, when he would come to her and they would have an intimate healing experience.

She waited for him in her room in anticipation. When he finally came, without saying a word, he lifted the nightdress off her. He stroked her naked body. He washed her with warm water, kissed her, then washed her again. Now he told her that God was on the way. Now everything would be fine once again. He placed fresh vegetable juice on the chest of drawers and told her she should drink it to cleanse her body for the journey ahead. He slipped his fingers gently through her hair and left the room, saying he would return shortly. She was to wait on the bed once she had drunk the juice.

Carla was in a bemused state of mind, and there was a strange tension in her belly. She went over to the chest of drawers, picked up the drink and began to sip it. But she hadn't drunk much when she felt an urge to vomit, and barely managed to reach a bowl before the green vegetable mess came straight back up. Carla was devastated. She had ruined everything. She tried to drink more of the green liquid, but her body simply wouldn't let her – knowing she would just bring it up again. She was ashamed – she so wanted to get better, and she desperately wanted to please Óttar, too. She carefully put the bowl and its contents, as well as the still almost-full glass of juice, into one of the drawers, and lay down on the bed. But Óttar didn't come back; he must have known she hadn't finished her preparation for the healing journey, she thought. She felt doomed.

She didn't know how long she had been lying there when she

heard the eldest girl cry out, calling for John. Carla didn't dare move. Was this all her fault? She began to weep quietly.

At that moment, the door to her room burst open and John stood there. When he saw her, he rushed over, put his arms around her and lifted her up.

'Are you all right?' he asked as he brushed away her tears.

'Forgive me, John,' was all she could say before losing consciousness.

The next morning she awoke to find the eldest girl sitting in a chair at her bedside, holding her hand. She wept with relief when Carla looked up at her, then helped her to dress and took her down to the living room. John was there, unkempt and out of sorts. He was delighted to see her and gestured for her to sit beside him. He looked her up and down for a long time, before asking her forgiveness for having invited the Devil into their sanctuary. The Devil had taken the two other girls who had fallen sick. John felt he had failed them, he said. And had failed her too. Then he shed tears. Carla was still confused and told John that Óttar would help them. John looked up into her eyes and spoke through his tears.

'Óttar is the Devil, and he's the one who has taken them,' he said.

After Óttar had left with the other girls, things changed at the farm. John never went anywhere other than to buy provisions. The house was falling into disrepair and John's connection with God seemed to have become infrequent, but still he promised to protect the three who remained with him.

Then Stephen was born. Beautiful Stephen. He brought joy to them all, such a robust and healthy child. Carla's life was so focused on him, she hardly noticed that John seemed to be fading slowly away. Carla and the other girls spent their days seeing to Stephen's needs, the house gradually falling apart around them.

❋

When Stephen was four years old, the eldest girl decided to move away. John made no objection, and even helped prepare her for her journey, giving her some money so she could find somewhere to live. But her departure seemed to affect John badly. What had been a slow decline in his health suddenly accelerated. And shortly afterwards, John was taken seriously ill. Carla and the other remaining girl nursed him, until he fell into a peaceful sleep and didn't wake up.

Shortly before his death, he had beckoned Carla to his side and asked her never to mention to anyone the arrival of the Devil, or his deeds. He had looked at her with caring eyes and assured her that the real truth was, she had never been affected by Devil's work. She had turned into a wonderful girl and a loving mother, he said. Now, after his passing, she would have to give Stephen a good, beautiful life, and she would do this by leaving behind in this house all the evil she'd experienced.

After his death, they discovered John had a significant amount of money, and the rent on the farm had been paid in cash some years in advance, so the owner of the place asked no questions of them. However, it must have got round that John had passed away, because the authorities began to be inquisitive about these very young girls living at a farm where an older man had just died. Carla and the other girl quickly decided to make themselves scarce, and taking the cash John had left them for just this purpose, they went their separate ways.

Carla ended up in Biwabik. She found work right away at a hotel. Her schooling had come to an end at the age of eleven, but she was well used to kitchen and cleaning work after her life at the farm. To begin with, she and Stephen lived in a small room in one of the hotel buildings. After she had managed to save enough money, she found her little house. She started out by renting it, and was finally able to buy it from the couple who owned it. She had made a good life for herself, and was immensely proud of Stephen, who'd grown up into a fine young man. He'd done well at high school, and gone away to college and after got himself a good job. But he still called her frequently and visited her regularly. So she felt there was a happy ending to her tale.

Carla had never before told anyone her whole story. She had only told parts of it, and then only in an edited version, brushed with brighter colours. Whenever she told people that she had lived as part of a religious group, some generally stopped asking questions, while others were keen to hear more. She gave the latter group a version that seemed innocent enough and demanded no further explanation. She'd learned that people had little understanding of how someone could be manipulated and brainwashed in the way she was. But Carla herself had, with time begun to understand what had happened to her. It was only as an adult that she learned that John's real name was Peter Adamsson. And she'd also discovered that he was wanted in California for abusing young girls.

Carla then made another discovery. The two girls who'd become sick at the same time as her were found dead of overdoses in Minneapolis not long after that fateful evening. According to the media, the girls were runaways who had become victims of narcotics after having been many years on the streets – the tragic but all-too-familiar fate of children with vulnerable backgrounds. But Carla knew the real story. And she was sure the other girls who had been at the farm now knew it too, wherever they were.

After Óttar left, John had suddenly stopped his religious efforts and the abusive 'connecting with God' sessions with the girls. After finding out that her two friends had died, Carla was certain that he had in fact suffered a nervous breakdown. He'd brought Óttar into those girls' lives, and that had led to their deaths – and nearly led to hers too. In his own twisted mind, he must have felt some kind of guilt.

Carla naturally knew now that Stephen was Óttar's child. He'd had no self-control and always came inside her when they had their 'spiritual' times together. John's abuse was of another nature, though, and it definitely ruled him out as the father.

In Carla's mind, however, there was no element of Óttar in her boy. Her bright, gentle and thoughtful little boy.

'He's nothing like him,' was the last thing she told Sigurdís, before they said their goodbyes, and Sigurdís headed out into the quiet night.

41

Sigurdís found a place to stay at a guest house right on the main street and not far from the statue of Honk the Elk. She was beginning to feel a fondness for the elk who had brought Carla to this place, showing her where to find the genuine and longed-for security that her young heart searched for.

A woman called Tammy showed her to a small room that was very different from Carla's home. It was crammed full of stuff – to the extent that it all melded into one big sensory overload. A floral doily adorned a table and on it stood a lamp with a large, frilled shade, next to a little statue of Honk the Elk. Next to the table stood a large armchair with floral upholstery. The bed was in a class of its own, piled high with cushions of all sorts. Patterns on top of patterns, as Dóra would have said. It bothered Sigurdís, but by now she was so tired that before long she quickly ceased to notice the many different flower motifs on everything in the room. The conversation with Carla, however, remained at the forefront of her mind. She had never before encountered anyone who had been through such experiences. There was nothing pretty about her own family backstory, but at least she and Einar had been surrounded by good people who had taken them in and became their foster parents after their parents were no longer there for them. Sigurdís had really liked Carla, a warm girlish-looking woman with a heartbreaking story to tell. Brave and strong, she had managed to come out the other side, living a peaceful life in this beautiful town, far away from her turbulent youth.

Sigurdís could hear her stomach rumbling, but couldn't even consider eating. Not after that. Good grief.

She sent Dóra a message to let her know that she was safe, but she was not up to chatting right now. How on earth could she talk about everyday stuff after hearing that story? She shivered at the thought of the New York nightlife weekend coming up. She was due to fly over there in two days, but what she really wanted to do was go home. Sigurdís decided to push these thoughts aside and try to get some sleep. It had been a long day, and the time difference was catching up with her.

The next morning she found Hank's diner. It wasn't easy to miss it on the little town's main street. He greeted her with a big smile and promised her the house eggs and bacon. The place was charming in its simplicity, with a scattering of tables and a long counter facing the row of coffee machines and cooler cabinets. In the middle of all this was a range where the chef prepared meals for everyone.

The food was wonderful, and Sigurdís shovelled down eggs, bacon, American pancakes, potatoes and grilled tomatoes with glee.

When she was done, she pushed her plate to the side and took out her computer. She started by searching for information on Peter Adamsson. His date of birth was given as 1958, so he had been eleven years older than Óttar and twenty-two years older than Carla. Carla was now just over forty, although she looked much the same age as Sigurdís. The thought of those abusers' hands touching the young, petite, girl that Carla had been made Sigurdís shudder. On a website database of old newspaper articles, she found some mentions of Peter Adamsson, relating how he had come from California, where he had abused a number of young girls, just as Carla had described.

How can these men just disappear into the throng then play the same games under a new name in another state? Sigurdís wondered in horror. Maybe it had been easier before the internet, and no doubt it had helped that he had a substantial amount of money – however he had obtained it.

After further searching, she discovered a report that added a lot of detail to the picture she was forming of this blackhearted man. It claimed he had been one of those who had taken part in abusing young people in a notorious religious movement that had called itself The Children of God, which had been first established in 1969. She could hardly believe her eyes when she read that this movement was still active, having changed its name more than a few times. She skimmed through a few interviews with young women who had spent part of their childhood within the movement, many of them left there by their parents to experience 'enlightenment', but who had ended up being abused by the older members. She understood now where Adamsson had learned the brainwashing techniques that Carla had described. He had certainly learned this sinister skill well during his time there.

She was absorbed in reading when she heard Hank's voice.

'Aren't you supposed to be on vacation? You shouldn't be so serious if that's the case. Coffee?'

Sigurdís smiled and said she preferred Diet Coke to coffee, even at ten in the morning. Hank laughed, and said that when you're on vacation, Coke for breakfast was just fine, but he hoped she didn't do it every day.

'So what is it you're reading that's putting such a sad look on your face?' he asked as he brought an ice-cold Coke and sat down next to her.

'News from around the world always has that effect,' she said shortly, not wanting to engage in conversation about what she was actually reading.

Hank looked serious and said that he understood exactly how she felt. He then embarked on a long tirade about the state of US politics, concluding that all these politicians were scoundrels who couldn't be trusted.

'But aren't you in local politics?' she asked, without thinking.

Hank grinned. 'Sure, but there isn't a lot of politics in that, except when the big operators want to get their hooks into the tourism business around here. That's when Hank's not the man the big boys want to have to face, believe me,' he said and laughed so heartily that Sigurdís couldn't help joining in.

She liked Hank and his big, loud personality. He left her to serve other customers, and as far as she could make out, they were practically all friends of his. Maybe that was only to be expected in such a small town, with its neighbourhood feel.

She turned back to her research and mulled over what she'd learned. And she couldn't get away from the fact that the conversation with Carla had convinced her that her theory was correct: the murder had nothing to do with money. The guilty person had to be someone much closer to Óttar. She was now certain of this and was determined to work out who it was who had ended the life of the disconcertingly multi-faceted Óttar. How could a man who seemed to have been unable to stop himself taking advantage of and manipulating people in such hideous ways have been able to get away with it for all these years? The answer undoubtedly lay in the skill with which he presented such a smooth, professional persona. And it seemed that, as well as being a sociopath, he was also exceptionally intelligent. Normal people don't expect that kind of behaviour from someone in his position, and with his charm and talents. Even lowlifes such as Peter, John, or whatever he called himself, had fallen for his patter. The only positive she could find in their interaction seemed to have been that Peter had stopped abusing young girls following his involvement with Óttar.

According to Carla, on his deathbed Peter had begged the girls to forgive him for having brought Óttar into their little world. He had explained to them how he and Óttar had spent time together after they encountered each other on one of the reservations, having long conversations about God and their dreams, and gradually their friendship had developed. It had appeared to Peter, from the way Óttar had talked, that they thought along the same lines, and he had been delighted to meet a young man with the same outlook on life as his own. When the exhausted Óttar had told him that he needed to take a break from his studies and to find a refuge from the outside world, Peter had not thought twice about helping him, and invited him to join the small community at the farm.

Sigurdís was starting to see a pattern. Óttar seemed to have the psychopath's knack of adapting himself to the people from whom he wanted something, showing interest and understanding until his prey believed that they had found a soul mate and placed complete trust in him. Well, these two had certainly made a fine pair of assholes when they had come together, she thought. Óttar had even managed to disgust Peter, which indicated that there had been some limits even to that man's sick mind. But where did Óttar's limits lie? Had there been any?

Sigurdís stood up and thanked Hank, before heading out to the car. She had meant to speak to Stephen, and maybe even other people who might have known Óttar, but after the conversation with Carla, she decided she wouldn't bother him. Stephen didn't need her stirring things up for him. She also didn't feel confident that she could talk to him without letting slip something that Carla had told her in confidence. If he needed to know any of this, then he ought to hear it from his mother. She wasn't sure that was advisable.

Why would he need to know? she thought. Having this knowledge would probably knock his legs from under him.

She set off towards the twin cities. She wanted to lose herself in the crowds of Minneapolis, where she would find herself somewhere quiet to go through everything and write a report detailing what she had discovered during this trip. She also hoped to be able to find some information about the two girls who had become pregnant by Óttar and who had been found dead in an empty, run-down house. She was excited, but a hell of a lot nervous at the same time, about giving Garðar an account of this crazy escapade of hers. He wouldn't be best pleased – and that was to say the least – but there was nothing to be done about that now. She felt she had nothing to lose. First she had to finish this girls' weekend. Then she had a task ahead of her – because the person she needed to meet next was in Iceland. A person who hadn't told them the whole truth.

42

Sigurdís had to admit to herself that the girls' trip to New York had done her good. Before meeting her friends, she had found time to write the report that set out everything Carla had told her, connecting the relevant people and Carla's information with what she already knew from the investigation about Óttar's life. Knowing she'd this done meant that she was free to relax, and she managed to laugh and let loose more than she had in a long time. Her batteries had been properly recharged. Dóra had even talked her into buying a dress.

'You need to show off that fab, toned body of yours!' Dóra had said, ushering her into a small shop in Little Italy.

Sigurdís was no spendthrift and took care to put savings aside. And now she'd mastered the art of travelling she was determined to use those savings to do it more; and next time she would take Einar along. He hadn't been abroad since the trip to Spain with Halla four years ago. They needed to spend more quality time together, and to build up a bank of shared memories unconnected to their childhood. That might turn out to be difficult though if Agnar were to continue trying to intrude into their lives. This thought reminded her that he was on his way to Iceland in a week's time. Anything to do with him didn't bode well. *What does he want from us?* Sigurdís wondered.

Their flight landed early on Tuesday morning and Sigurdís decided to go straight to the station to check in with her colleagues. She wasn't sure just how badly Garðar would react when he found out what had really taken her to America. But she tried not to dwell on this concern, and decided that the worst that could have happened in her absence would be that they'd uncovered some more convincing evidence against Guðmundur Kaldal, and that all her work was wasted and she was simply mistaken. At least, she had done everything expected of her, and more, to try and solve the case.

'You can't win if you don't buy the ticket,' Halla had always said to her and Einar, encouraging them to follow their dreams. 'If you don't make an effort, then you can be sure of one thing: nothing will change – and that's even more of a loss than trying. If you make the effort and there's no big return, then at least you've learned something that will be a benefit to you in your future endeavours.'

Sigurdís smiled fondly to herself as she thought of Halla. They had been so incredibly lucky that she had been able to step in for them. She was reliable and trustworthy, with an open heart. Halla had changed the courses of their lives when she had taken them in. She loved them unconditionally, as if they were her own children, and she and Einar had never doubted that love for a second.

The investigation team were sitting in the incident room. There was silence and they were all engrossed in paper documents or computer screens, so nobody noticed as she entered the room. A mess of pizza boxes, cans and cups, and sweet wrappers lay here and there.

'It's like a teenager's bedroom in here,' Sigurdís announced to the group. 'The only thing missing is empty energy-drink cans,' she grinned.

'Hey, Sigurdís! Back from Trumpland? Good to see you!'

Unnar got to his feet and came over to her. 'Did you have a good vacation?'

She was about to reply, when she saw Garðar stand up and ask her for a private word. They went to his office and he asked her to shut the door behind her.

'Did you manage to have a good time, Sigurdís?' he asked.

She told him about the New York part of the trip. She was trying to summon the courage to tell him about the conversation with Carla, when he took the conversation in another direction.

'I wanted a word with you about your father—'

'Could you stop referring to him as my father?' Sigurdís interrupted. 'I'd be happier if you just call him Agnar.'

Garðar was silent for a moment, and agreed; Agnar hadn't been much of a father.

'We have a week until he arrives in Iceland. Not that there's anything to say he'll actually catch the flight,' he said, then hesitated before continuing. 'It's a one-way ticket he bought, so it seems like he is preparing to stay once he's back here.'

Sigurdís stared at him, a feeling of horror gripping her chest. She dropped into a chair. 'What do you think we should do, Garðar? He'll wreck our lives. He's our very own fucking Voldemort.' She looked into Garðar's eyes and saw that they were welling up. That made all of Sigurdís's defences collapse, and she burst into tears. 'How can I tell Halla and Einar all of this? Einar thinks it's all his fault that the old man is coming back, because he replied to his messages. I tried to tell him that it didn't make any difference, and that he'd obviously made up his mind to come before he got in touch. Like it's his God-given right to keep fucking with everyone and everything around him.'

Garðar placed a hand on her shoulder and squeezed gently. 'I will be by your side when you break the news to Halla and Einar. I'm here for you this time around – I want you to know that.'

When Sigurdís had wiped away her tears and pulled herself together, she went to find Unnar. He stood by a window overlooking the ocean, his hands in his pockets in deep thought. As he turned around their eyes met and he gave her a warm smile, before welcoming her back once again. She pushed aside the tingling feeling she was experiencing at seeing him again, and decided she needed to get him out of the building so they could have some privacy. She needed to share with him what she had learned from her conversation with Carla and get his feedback on the possible next steps.

They went to sit in a coffee house not far from the busy Hlemmur bus terminal opposite the police station. This place was one of the hipster cafés where everything on offer was organic and fair trade, and it had a reputation for its wonderful sourdough bread. The owners had managed to tastefully create a pleasant feel to the place, fitting it out with an assortment of mismatched old furniture. They sat down in armchairs either side of a small table in a quiet corner.

Unnar sat in thought once Sigurdís had told him the whole story of the conversation with Carla and the newspaper articles she had dug up concerning the deaths of the two girls. He hadn't even touched the coffee while he listened to her; it had just cooled down on the table in front of him.

He cleared his throat then stood up, looking as though he didn't know what to do with himself. She worried he was about to walk out.

'So who was this man? Or, maybe the question is, what was this man,' he said, and looked at her intently as he sat back down, pulling his chair closer to hers. 'I don't know what to say, really. You're full of surprises, Sigurdís. I told you not to go, but you didn't let that stop you. You went hunting down the answers like a dog with a bone.' He shook his head slowly. 'I can't condone what you did, I really can't. But I reckon the rest of us could learn a thing or two from you. And after listening to what you've dug up, well ... *Respect* is all I can say to that.' He gave her a big grin. 'Because I reckon there really is something in what you've found out. We still haven't been able to nail this on Guðmundur to the prosecutor's satisfaction. I think he's just a broken man, and while he would've loved to get his hands on Óttar, I don't believe he was anywhere near him that night.'

They both reflect on the unfortunate man who was now cooling his heels in custody.

Unnar ordered himself a fresh cup of coffee and sipped it as he spoke.

'You know, Sigurdís, for a guy like me, who was brought up with plenty of love and attention from both parents, it's difficult to get a feeling for dishonesty and hateful behaviour like this when it's hidden behind such a pleasant façade. So I think this perceptiveness of yours is no accident. You've been unconsciously trained to read more deeply into situations like this than most of us can. You latch on to things I barely notice, even tiny details, and then put it all together to form a picture. I don't think this is something that can be taught. You have to learn it through the challenges life has sent your way – just like you've done, unfortunately.'

Sigurdís had never found it easy to accept compliments. And it felt especially difficult to hear them when they were directed at characteristics she had developed through her challenging early years.

'I don't know how grateful I should be for this kind of training,' she said shortly.

'Apologies, Sigurdís. I didn't want to drag you back to the bad times. I just wanted to point out how much strength there is inside you. I don't think you realise it.'

She glanced over to him and smiled. 'Thank you, I guess. I'm not sure everyone will see this in the same positive light as you, and I have no idea how I'm going to tell Garðar all this.'

Unnar smiled encouragingly. 'What's done is done. But most importantly, you have information now that he needs to hear.'

They stood up, and as they walked to the door he laid a hand lightly across her shoulders, pulling her a little closer to him.

'Now go and tell Garðar the whole thing. You're throwing him a lifeline, because the case has hit a dead end. I'll back you up – and your theory – with him and the rest of the team, if you need me to.'

An electric charge had passed through Sigurdís's body when she felt the touch of Unnar's hands, and an image from that dream flashed through her mind.

She coughed, pulled her phone from her pocket and studied it, pretending she was checking a message. These feelings of hers towards Unnar were becoming increasingly frequent. Sigurdís valued his friendship and their working relationship highly, and knew that she would have to cool down these feelings if she didn't want to lose him or make things awkward between them.

43

Halla and Einar were waiting for Sigurdís and Garðar when they arrived at their home on Háaleitisbraut – a spacious seventies terraced house with a small front yard, neatly kept. They both came to the door, clearly anticipating bad news. They hadn't been able to hide their astonishment when Sigurdís had called to warn them that she and Garðar needed to speak to them, together. Halla had done her best to get out of her what was up, but Sigurdís had got around it by saying that she was needed at work, and put the phone down.

Halla was cold towards Garðar, but courteous as she invited them in. Sigurdís could sense her animosity, even though Halla did everything she could to conceal her feelings. She hadn't forgiven Garðar for the way things had gone years ago.

Sigurdís suggested they sat down in the kitchen. This was her favourite place in the whole house. She and Halla had sat here many times over the years, to talk things through. *That kitchen table has to go. It knows too much,* she decided, laughing inwardly at the thought. In fact, she would never let Halla part with the table. She knew every inch of it, every tiny scratch. She had spent so much time sitting there, running her nails over the pattern in the pale wood, shifting things aside so she could look into Halla's eyes as they talked. Halla had seen her go from the top to the bottom of her emotional range, and had never failed to comfort and support her all the way. She had also scolded her, praised her and given her sympathy at this table. Now she and Garðar would have to sit down and give her and Einar the news over this table. But it was the place where problems were tackled and solutions found, she told herself.

To buy a little time, Sigurdís offered to make coffee, or get them something else to drink. Nobody accepted, and they all sat down around the kitchen table and waited for her to join them.

Then Garðar forged ahead, and explained that he had been keeping tabs on Agnar for some time, that he hadn't made direct contact with him and had no desire to do so, but had taken it upon himself to make sure he knew of his movements. He told them everything he had already told Sigurdís, without mentioning that he had kept her informed this whole time. He clearly didn't want to cause her any more problems. She was grateful to him for this, because she knew Einar and Halla would resent her for keeping everything from them for this long.

When he told them that Agnar planned to arrive in Iceland in a week's time, Halla gasped. 'Good God, what does he want to come here for? Can't he leave these poor children in peace?' She reached out to pull Einar close to her, as if she was frightened that Agnar could appear at any moment and whisk him away. Einar sat in silence, his hands under the table, staring downward, gazing at the table's surface, just as Sigurdís had done so many times.

Sigurdís stretched across the table and grasped their arms, saying that Garðar would ensure their safety.

Halla's gaze was piercing as she glared at him. 'Yes, he ought to know how dangerous this man is. Considering how hard it was to get him to take this seriously back then,' she said from between clenched teeth.

Garðar remained impassive, and told them that he had taken measures to ensure that Agnar would be watched carefully while he was in the country, and that he would also ensure that a patrol car kept an eye on their home, as well as on Sigurdís's flat. In addition, he had ordered security systems to be installed in their homes over the next few days. There would also be panic alarms for each of them, which were fitted with a location system so a car could be dispatched as soon as the buttons were pressed. He emphasised that they should never be without them.

'No need for a security system at my place,' Sigurdís said firmly. 'I'll stay in my old room here until this all blows over.'

Halla clearly didn't know what to say, and still held Einar tight. Sigurdís saw that he had begun to tremble.

Garðar coughed. 'I won't let anything happen to you,' he said in a low voice. 'I promise. Nothing at all. I'm so sorry that I failed you when you came to me, Halla. I—'

He was interrupted by Einar shooting to his feet and shouting, 'It wasn't your fault, Garðar.' His voice quavered. 'He was the one who made the decision to beat our mother. He was the one who ran his household with an iron fist – and even used it directly on his children. You didn't do this. He did.' He fell silent, and seemed to be about to break into tears. 'And it's my fault that he got riled up when he was in touch with me. Because I answered him. I should never have replied. So it's my job to fix this.'

He let himself sink back into his chair, and bent his head over the table.

Sigurdís stood up and went round to him, wrapping her arms around him and whispering in his ear.

'Never ever take any blame for his actions. The blame is all Agnar's, both then and now, not yours or anyone else's. We'll get through this if we stick together. We have to show him that he has no place in our lives.'

'And this time I'm with you,' Garðar added once more. 'All the way.'

✷ 44 ✷

As she and Garðar left Halla's house, Sigurdís knew she could no longer keep quiet about what she had found out in America. It had been weighing on her and he would find out soon anyway what she'd been up to. So as soon as they were in the car she started her narrative.

By the time they reached the station, she was halfway through her account. Garðar hadn't interrupted her once, the whole time. Now, he switched off the engine, turned to face her, and told her to continue. Sigurdís had never before seen him so lost for words. His expression had been neutral as he drove, but now she could see the tension in the muscles of his jaw as he clenched his teeth and breathed deeply.

'I don't know what to say, Sigurdís,' he said finally, just as Unnar had done. 'I want to give you an earful for going off on your own without saying anything to me. This is totally in-appropriate and goes against every rule of police work. There are reasons for all the procedures, and certainly they don't allow for you or anyone else to play some kind of game of Dirty Harry.' He let that sink in for a moment, fixing her with a hard stare. Then he looked forward, out through the windscreen, and sighed. 'On the other hand, I think you're on to something.' He cleared his throat. 'I have to put up my hands and admit that it feels like I've completely lost control of this investigation. We've made no progress on Guðmundur and to be honest, we've hit a wall.'

He shifted in the driver's seat, put both hands on the wheel and pushed, pressing himself back into the seat.

'OK. This is the way we'll play it. Even though you went rogue, I'll back you up because I don't want you to get a black mark for this. Hell, you might be on the trail that we've been looking for all this time.'

They got out of the car, and as they went inside and climbed the stairs to the incident room, Garðar suggested that she take a coffee break and get ready for a meeting with Erla. He wasn't sure it was the moment yet to inform the rest of the team. And he told her to let him know of all her movements from now on. He was responsible for her safety, even though he was gradually realising that she was quite capable of taking care of herself.

She gave him a guilty smile and promised there would be no more solo escapades.

She was walking away when he called out to her, 'Hey, Dirty Harry!' She turned, and he continued, 'I also think we need to talk to the mother and the sister again, Thrúður and Stefanía. They know more than they're giving away.'

✳ 45 ✳

Sigurdís had prepared carefully for her conversation with Erla. Garðar had been very supportive and had given her some guidance on interview techniques that could come in useful. Although this wasn't a formal interrogation, there were particular methods for extracting information during a conversation. When Sigurdís was nervous she tended to be impulsive and bombarded people with questions that could make them defensive right off the bat. She couldn't do that this time. This interview was the single most important of her career so far.

She was going through her notes at her desk when Unnar sat down next her. 'It's important that you manage this well, as we don't want the case to come to grief on some technicality,' Unnar said thoughtfully. He had offered to come with her, but they, and Garðar, had agreed that Erla was most likely to open up if Sigurdís were to meet her alone. 'I'll be by the phone, so call me if you need anything or if you could do with some support.'

Erla had told Sigurdís to come and meet her at her home. It wasn't easy to find a parking spot near Erla's home in the western part of the city. She parked outside the University Cinema, and walked briskly to Viðimelur. It was starting to get dark already, with gusts of autumn wind and rain, and she was practically soaked through by the time she stood at Erla's door.

Every light in the apartment looked to be switched off and the curtains were drawn across the windows. Sigurdís cursed to herself, certain that Erla wasn't home, and was surprised when the door swung open almost as soon as she had pressed the doorbell. Erla stood in the dark, looking back at her, and invited her in. She was nothing like the Erla Sigurdís had met previously. She had lost a great deal of weight. Her hair was greasy and pulled into an untidy ponytail. In the light cast by the streetlamps outside, Sigurdís could see black patches under her eyes. She wore a shapeless grey T shirt, black leggings and a red dressing gown.

Erla went ahead of her into the living room, and stood by the window, arms folded, as Sigurdís walked in.

'Sorry for the state of me,' she said in a low voice, indicating her clothes. 'I haven't been to work for a few weeks. My partners wanted me to take time off, sick leave.'

Sigurdís looked around the apartment without responding. It was in the same state of disarray as Erla herself. A duvet lay bunched up on the sofa, glasses containing varying amounts of water stood on the table and there was one plate, on which lay a single slice of stale, untouched bread. The same picture Sigurdís had seen in Erla's office lay on the table – the smiling girl. This one wasn't in a frame, but lay unprotected on the table, a little creased.

'What was your cousin's name?' Sigurdís asked.

'Anna Guðrún,' Erla said as she turned to look at her with empty eyes. 'She was the other half of me. After she was gone I did everything to live for both of us.'

Erla took a seat in a chair facing the sofa and gestured for Sigurdís to sit down. Sigurdís moved the duvet aside and sat down. She was nervous, painfully aware of how important this conversation might be. She wasn't used to questioning people in depth, and wished she had some of Garðar's long experience, or even Unnar's. It would have come in useful under these circumstances.

Erla looked at her in silence, and it was welcome. Sigurdís used it to calm her thoughts, knowing that she needed to take her time, as Erla seemed to be in no state to be pressed too hard. After a moment, Sigurdís felt that she was ready.

'I've been to Minnesota, Erla,' she said gently.

Erla stood up, came across to the sofa and sat next to Sigurdís, with her back against the armrest and her legs folded beneath her. She pulled the duvet towards her and held it tight against her belly.

'Then you know that I spoke to Carla,' she said at last, and Sigurdís could see Erla tremble.

'Yes Erla, I know now.'

After Carla had finished telling Sigurdís her story, she had confessed that Sigurdís hadn't been the first Icelander to call her. Someone claiming to be Óttar's girlfriend had contacted her earlier in the year.

'Why didn't you tell us that you spoke to Carla?'

Erla's shoulders slumped. Sigurdís wasn't certain of how much Erla knew about Carla and Óttar, or even Stephen, and it was important to find out.

'I can see you're not feeling well, Erla. This is clearly weighing heavily on you. So how about you just tell me what you know? I have plenty of time, so go at your own pace.'

Erla looked at her with eyes full of doubt, and then it seemed that something inside her gave way and she began to tell her story.

Last winter it had seemed to Erla that her life could not be better. Work was going well and her boyfriend was perfect. He would turn fifty in July and she wanted to do something special for him, so she decided to bring people together for a surprise party. There was another reason behind her wanting to do this: she wanted to develop a better understanding of him, get to know his friends and not least, the people he had known during the course of his life. She took the idea to Þrúður and Stefanía. They both approved of it and promised not to say a word and also to help her organise the party. So it came as a surprise when they began to discourage her when she told them that she wanted to find some friends and colleagues from his school years, especially from his time in America. They even tried to tell her that it was only relatively recently that he had become gregarious. Erla found this dubious, somehow, and couldn't help starting to dig for more information. But she found it difficult to find any friends of his from school, and only tracked down a few people who had been in the same year as him at the Commercial College.

Erla made herself more comfortable on the sofa and pulled her knees up to her chin. Her arms were wrapped around her legs and the duvet had slipped so that one end lay on the floor. She rocked to and fro a little as she continued her narrative.

At around this time, when she was looking for old friends of Óttar's, she arrived at his flat a little ahead of him one evening. It always looked like a showcase apartment to her – everything in its place – so she was surprised to see a note on the counter next to the bathroom basin. He had written a name, Stephen, and a phone number with a +1 prefix, indicating that it was a US number. She took the slip of paper, put it on the kitchen worktop and asked Óttar when he finally arrived home who it was. Óttar glanced at the piece of paper, and replied with a cheerful smile that this was an old friend from his university years in Minnesota. He had found the note in an old briefcase and meant to throw it away, but had forgotten as he rushed out the door that morning.

When he went off to his study to put away his briefcase and the documents he had brought home from work, Erla pounced on the opportunity and snapped a photo of the number with her phone, convinced that she had found a friend of his in

America who would want to be here for his birthday. A few minutes later, she noticed that the slip of paper was gone from the kitchen counter.

A few weeks afterwards, when she was preparing a guest list, she started to make calls, and included the number she had found at Óttar's place. A young man answered, and confirmed that his name was Stephen, but he didn't know anyone called Óttar. Erla pressed him, telling him that she had found his number in Óttar's apartment, explaining why she was calling, and Stephen had told her it would be best to speak to his mother. He gave her Carla's number, then quickly hung up.

At this point Erla seemed so overcome that Sigurdís didn't dare take her eyes off her. She was concerned that Erla would faint, harm herself, or just crumble and blow away like dust. After a short pause, Erla reached for one of the glasses of water on the table and sipped at it. Her hand shook so violently that the water slopped out. Sigurdís reached for the glass, gently took it from her and placed it on the table. Erla again bunched the duvet in her arms and held it tight as she gazed at Sigurdís from eyes that brimmed with tears.

'You know about the relationship with Carla, right?'

Sigurdís nodded and put a hand on her arms, stroking it gently with her thumb.

'Yes, I do now. But it would help if you could tell me what she told you.'

Erla had been more cheerful than usual the day she had called Carla. This was in the middle of May, a beautiful spring day with summer approaching. She had concluded a large merger, and that morning the competition authority had given it the green light. She had clinked glasses with her colleagues and clients, then, when everyone had gone home, she decided to stay on at the office and finally put some more effort into organising the birthday party. She felt guilty over having left this unfinished, and was concerned that she had left it too late for people to organise a trip to Iceland to celebrate an old friend's birthday, if she were even to find any of Óttar's old friends.

The effects of the prosecco they had drunk earlier helped her prepare her pitch. She hadn't expected Carla to pick up the phone on the second ring, so she took a deep breath and apologised for troubling her before going on to the reason for the call. Carla had been silent, before saying that she knew nobody who had been at university with Óttar. Erla found Carla oddly cold, and had the feeling that she had come up against a barrier. She then told Carla that she was Óttar's fiancée and that he was such a wonderful person that she really wanted to do something special for his fiftieth birthday. None of this had any effect on Carla, who said again that she couldn't help her.

'Then why was your son's phone number among Óttar's things?' Erla asked, almost without meaning to.

Carla hadn't answered the question, but asked after a long pause if she and Óttar had any children. This had taken Erla by surprise, and she replied that they were childless, for the moment, at least. Carla said she was relieved to hear it. This time it was Erla's turn to be silent. For a moment she was lost for words.

'Why do you say that?' she asked.

Carla took a deep breath. 'I can hear that you're very fond of Óttar,' she said, 'but there are clearly things you don't know.' Erla protested, asking what Carla meant. There was silence on the line for a moment then Carla took another deep breath. 'Before I tell you any more,' she said, 'I want you to promise you won't mention a word of this to him. I don't want any repercussions that might affect my son. I also won't tell anyone about this conversation.'

Trembling, Erla gave Carla her word.

Then Carla proceeded to tell her that Óttar wasn't the man

he appeared to be, and she should be wary of him. This angered Erla, but Carla continued and told her how Óttar had treated young girls during his time in Minnesota. She told her to prepare herself well and to end the relationship before he left her hurt. He wasn't a good man. Carla wanted nothing on her conscience. She knew, at least, that she had warned Erla as soon as she'd discovered she was in a relationship with him.

'Are we talking about the same man?' Erla gasped.

'Yes. If he has Stephen's number, then there's no doubt.'

While she had related all this, Erla had slid down to the floor and was now sitting with her back against the sofa and her knees against the heavy table. She had pulled the duvet down with her and still held it crushed against her chest. It was clear that her misery wouldn't allow her to sit still. Her anxiety seemed to be like oil burning beneath her skin. A feeling Sigurdís knew all too well.

Sigurdís decided it was best to join her on the floor and sat next to her so that their shoulders touched.

'Then I realised that Óttar was Stephen's father,' Erla said, her voice quivering as she turned to look at Sigurdís. 'Carla was thirteen when he got her pregnant. Thirteen!'

She gasped for breath, and buried her face in the duvet to smother a scream. Sigurdís placed an arm around her shoulders, but Erla raised her head and shook it off.

'Please don't ... I can't handle being touched. It feels just revolting. I slept with that man.' She shuddered at the thought. 'I even slept with him after that phone call.'

They sat for a while without a word being said. Sigurdís couldn't imagine how it must feel to make such a discovery about someone so close; someone you trusted. But she had to ask why Erla hadn't confronted Óttar after that call.

'There was something else Carla said that made me need to figure some things out before I could do that,' Erla said in a voice so low that Sigurdís could barely hear her. She longed to know what was coming, but she tried to remain impassive as she waited for her to continue. 'She asked me if, when we were lying there together after sex, he called me his sweet, or even his whole bowl of sugar.'

✳ 46 ✳

Erla's cousin, Anna Guðrún, had moved from Höfn to Reykjavík when she was thirteen. Anna Guðrún hadn't been happy to move and made life difficult for her mother, who had decided to make a home in the capital after splitting up with Erla's uncle and starting a relationship with a new man. Erla remembered how happy Anna's mother had been. Erla's mother had said that her new partner was a good man and had been pleased for her former sister-in-law, as they had always been good friends. Anna Guðrún's and Erla's parents all remained on good terms after the amicable divorce had been finalised, but Anna Guðrún never found her footing in the city, and found it difficult to start a new school, meet new friends and get to know her step-father. Her mother was also deeply engrossed in her new partner and often went travelling with him, frequently leaving Anna Guðrún at home alone – as parents often did in those days.

Erla and Anna Guðrún spoke regularly and the bond between them remained strong. Anna Guðrún confided in her that she had made new friends who weren't at the same school. She had got to know them at a concert in the Hljómskála gardens close to the town hall. She had gone there on her own to see the popular band, GusGus. The kids were sitting not far from her and had asked her to come and join their group. They were drinking and offered her some, which she accepted. After that she spent a lot of time with them, and her calls to Erla became less frequent. Sometime later, Anna Guðrún's mother called Erla's in tears, saying she suspected that these youngsters were messing about with drugs, and that Anna Guðrún had been caught up in it. Finally she asked if Erla could come for a visit to help her re-establish the relationship with her daughter, who had now taken to disappearing for days at a time. Anna Guðrún's father was a seaman and away for long periods, so he wasn't involved in any of this – although he was preparing an extended time at home so that he could support the two of them and spend time with his daughter.

When Erla arrived in Reykjavík she was met by a completely different Anna Guðrún. She was wearing a short floral dress, with army boots and a leather jacket. She was no less beautiful, with her long dark hair and dark eyes. The change was more in her personality. She was restless and impatient, and gave the impression that she wanted to be anywhere but near her cousin. Erla had been hurt by her cousin's behaviour towards her, and asked her mother to buy her a bus ticket so she could come home earlier than planned.

A few days later, when Erla was at home in bed and about to fall asleep, her phone rang.

'Heeey, my darling,' Anna Guðrún had slurred. 'I'm sooo happy, I have to share this with you. I met a guy. Mister Sweet. He's so good-looking, and he's nice and smart. I'm learning so much from him. I've never been so happy, and we're going to be together for eeeever.'

A few months later Anna Guðrún was dead. She was found in an alley. An autopsy showed she had taken an overdose. And that she was eight weeks pregnant.

Erla was devastated. She and her mother went straight to Reykjavík where they stayed with Anna Guðrún's mother. Anna Guðrún's room was exactly as she had left it. One evening Erla sneaked in there and lay on her bed. She desperately wished for

Anna Guðrún to come back. She could smell her in the pillow and the duvet, in the sheet. She stretched out and that was when she found the diary. It had been under the mattress.

Now, still sitting on the floor, Erla reached under the sofa and took out an old diary. It was blue, with a broken clasp. She flipped through the pages to the middle and handed it to Sigurdís to read.

12.03.1995
Met Mr Sweet. Tall, good-looking and smart. He saved my life on Friday, when I was freezing to death downtown. Let me sit in his car and we went to a drive-in place for a burger and fries. I wolfed it down. Looked up and felt a bit stupid. He just laughed, wiped some cocktail sauce off my lip and pushed my hair away from my face. He's a dreamboat!

20.03.1995
Mr Sweet asked me to come for a ride around town. We talked for ages and then he asked if I'd like to come to his place, where it was warmer and more comfortable. He said I'm beautiful. I didn't believe him. Then he said he'd like to show me so I would believe him. It was the best night ever! I love him!

25.03.1995
I have butterflies in my stomach all day, every day. He wants to be with me all the time. Me!! I feel so good.
Mum is so happy I'm smiling more. So she's stopped smothering me with all her worries. And she's giving me more space too. Space to live my life and be with him. My Mr Sweet.

03.04.1995
Mum is leaving for her trip tomorrow. I can't wait. I can be with Mr Sweet the whole weekend!!

14.04.1995
I'm not hanging around with Kiddi, Jóna and that crowd anymore. They just want to keep me doing shitty stuff. They aren't real friends. Mr Sweet is everything I need. He's brilliant. He's my future. He studied in America. We can't tell anyone about us until I'm eighteen. Mum would go crazy if I told her about him. She doesn't understand that age doesn't matter when you're in love. Mr Sweet. Mr Sweet. Mr Sweet. Mr Sweet! He's so good to me. He strokes me and cuddles me. Sometimes he says I'm the one that's sweet – so sweet I'm his whole bowl of sugar!

30.04.1995
We sat together by the sea last night. We saw a ship sailing slowly into the harbour. All lit up in the dark, it looked like a circus ship, with a string of lights hanging between the masts just like the lights between the tent poles under the big top. He was sad. He's never sad. He told me it was a trawler coming in to land its catch. Trawlers are no circus ships. They take dads away from their children. I put my arms around him. We held each other tight. He promised he'd never leave me.

03.05.1995
I'm in love. In love. We're going to have a great life together. Mr Sweet says such lovely things about our future. A future full of happiness. I'm counting the days until we can live together. I've had enough of this place. I have to get out of here. To him. To find peace. With him. He says our souls will become one.

15.05.1995
He's going to take me away from here. He says I'm his girl, his beautiful girl. I lie and listen as he whispers God's word in my ear. I just shiver with joy. I give myself up to him. Every bit of me is his. We're one before God.

Sigurdís read one more entry, which were also the final words this young girl wrote, and she shuddered. She closed the diary and placed it on the table.

'Do you know many men who call little girls their sweet, or their bowl of sugar?' Erla asked, and her eyes flashed.

Sigurdís said nothing, but thought of how the diary entries had changed, how the young girl's own voice had become progressively weaker, overpowered. By him. She sat in silence as she heard Erla relate how hearing those words Carla had said to her on the phone had prompted her to put two and two together. That day, Erla had thanked Carla, crawled under her desk and huddled there in a foetal position the whole night long. Towards morning she had hurried home to check Anna Guðrún's diary. But she still doubted that there was a connection. Her Óttar wasn't that kind of man ... was he?

Sigurdís sat staring into empty space. Could Óttar have come home after finishing his studies in Minnesota and played the same game all over again? The final entry in the diary sat firmly in her mind. This couldn't be a coincidence, not taking everything into account; the language used to manipulate a young girl who was still a child.

Erla was on her feet, staring out of the living-room window.

'I acted as if nothing was wrong. I was in denial. I realise that now. This all seemed so farfetched. So beyond belief. Nobody acts like that. He knew all about Anna Guðrún and how important she had been to me. I'd told him. I couldn't believe that he could be with me if he was this "Mr Sweet" – no one is that evil. I tried to interpret everything he did, lay with him and called him cute names, and waited for him to call me his sweet, his bowl of sugar. But he never did.' She hesitated before continuing. 'The evening before his birthday he asked me to go with him out to the east and walk along the beach from Eyrabakki to Stokkseyri. We went further than we did usually, and sat down on a rock. He got a phone call and I sat there and looked out at the beautiful evening sunlight. When I took my phone out to take a picture, I saw that I had a message. A message from Carla. She sent me copies of newspaper reports about the two girls who were found after taking overdoses in Minneapolis. I don't remember much after that. I just remember that I told him that I knew about Carla and Stephen. He looked back at me in terror and that was when I knew. It was all true.'

Erla collapsed to her knees in front of the window.

'Did he choose me because of this? Why did this man come into my life? I can't take any more, Sigurdís. I'm so sorry I didn't tell you all this right away. I couldn't do it. I just couldn't,' she cried out hysterically.

After Guðmundur Kaldal Brjánsson was released, Sigurdís saw an interview with him online. He was shown standing outside a neat apartment block in Kópavogur, arm in arm with a young man the news article said was his son. In his interview, Guðmundur said that he was naturally relieved to be free, and bore no grudge against the police for all the months in custody. He said he had been off his head on the night in question, completely out of control, and unable to recall his own movements. He had lived with the anger towards anyone and anything for so long that he had lost sight of the important things in life. Now a new life was ahead of him and the first step was treatment for his alcohol addiction.

'Good for you, Guðmundur,' Sigurdís said to herself when she had finished reading.

After their conversation, Sigurdís had helped Erla get dressed, and had called Garðar. He had arrived to pick them up and bring them down to the station, where Erla confessed to everything in a formal interview. One of her colleagues from the legal practice had been at her side, representing her. Sigurdís felt a deep sympathy for her and tried to imagine what she would have done under similar circumstances, and not least among these was what she would have liked to have done to Agnar.

She went back to the incident room, where her colleagues were putting away documents and taking down the boards. A smiling Elín thanked her for all her work during the investigation. And Unnar came over to her and draped a hand over her shoulders. Sigurdís flushed as he whispered in her ear, 'You're a natural, Sigurdís. I told you so.'

Once everything had been cleared away Unnar suggested they go out for a stiff Diet Coke. Sigurdís wanted nothing more – she'd been longing to spend more time with Unnar – but it would have to wait. She would need all her strength for the days to come. Agnar was on his way to Iceland and she meant to stay close to Einar and Halla until it was clear what he was looking for or until Garðar could persuade him to head back to Denmark.

Garðar was deeply appreciative that Sigurdís had got to the bottom of the case. The whole story had left them both with a bad taste in their mouths. Sigurdís admitted to Garðar that for a moment it had occurred to her to tell Erla that her confession could remain a secret between the two of them, and that she should go on living as she had done, for the two of them, herself and Anna Guðrún. Garðar in turn had admitted with a smile that he had often had similar feelings during difficult interviews. It was just part of doing a challenging job, he said.

'I'm proud of you, Sigurdís. There's a real future for you here,' he told her. 'And I owe you an apology: I should have listened more carefully to what you had to say. I'll remember to do that next time you tell me I'm wrong.' And he gave her a sly grin.

She had already decided that her next step would be to become properly qualified, and she had had her eye on a university where she could major in criminal psychology. As soon as the storm around Agnar's arrival had passed, she would be sending in her application.

✳ 48 ✳

Sigurdís was asleep at Halla's house when her phone rang. Agnar had been in the country for two days now, and with the uncertainty they all felt, she was more comfortable being close to Halla and Einar. But they had heard nothing from him yet. Her colleagues were keeping watch on the house on Háaleitisbraut and there had been no sign of him.

It was Unnar calling. She sat up in bed and asked hoarsely if he was missing her already. But she heard from his response that this was no social call.

'Sigurdís, I'm on Hátún – at your mother's building. We were called out to an incident.'

Her eyes were instantly wide and she felt a knot of fire deep inside her.

'I, well...' Unnar stumbled over his words. 'Look, Sigurdís, there's a dead man here who looks like he's jumped or fallen from a balcony or from the roof. We don't know yet. His passport was on him ... It's ... it's Agnar Jónsson.'

Sigurdís sat frozen for a moment before she leaped from the bed and ran along the passage, through the TV room and into the hall. She yanked open a door.

'Einar!'

17.05.1995

There's life inside me. His life. Our life. He caressed me and washed me all over when I told him the news. His hands passed over every part of me with the flannel. He whispered words of love to me the whole time. I don't have to worry about anything anymore. He'll look after me. Soon we'll be one combined soul.

ACKNOWLEDGEMENTS

I am so grateful that my husband, Bjarni M. Bjarnason, encouraged me to start writing, kicking off this new and exciting journey in my life. Being an author himself, he is my sturdiest support when the writer's angst consumes my mind!

I am grateful for the love and support I received from Pétur Már Ólafsson, my publisher in Iceland, and from Bjarni Þorsteinsson, my editor there. Their patience is out of this world.

In the UK I have been in such good hands. My agent, David H. Headley, Karen Sullivan, my publisher, and West Camel, my editor, are simply the best. Thank you all for being there for me, and thank you also to Quentin Bates for bringing the story to life in a new language.

Finally I need to express my gratitude to you, my readers: a sincere thank you for reading my work, and a huge thank you for all your wonderful feedback.